I0659673

The Summer of WEiRD HAROLD

Eric Walker Williams

Culicidae
PRESS, LLC
culicidaepress.com

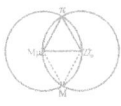

Austin | Gainesville | Lafage | Biarritz

Culicidae Press, LLC
918 5th Street
Ames, IA 50010
USA
www.culicidaepress.com

editor@culicidaepress.com

Culicidae
PRESS, LLC
culicidaepress.com

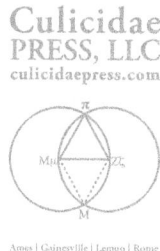

Ames | Gainesville | Lemgo | Rome

THE SUMMER OF WEIRD HAROLD

For more information, please visit www.culicidaepress.com or the author's website at www.ericwalkerwilliams.com

ISBN-13:   978-1-941892-25-1

ISBN-10:   1-941892-25-6

Cover design ©2016 by Kylin Schoeff
Interior layout ©2016 by polytekton.com

For Mom and Dad

1

~ ~ ~ ~ ~ ~ ~

Not so far away there's a quiet little place where the sun always shines, the water stays warm all year and your neighbors want to kill you.

This was going to be harder than I thought. I didn't want the lake to sound like the setting of a horror movie. There were no chainsaws or shapeless blobs lurking in the shallows. Wait a minute, I guess there was a chainsaw. A chainsaw, yes, but no blobs. Still, writing about everything that happened to my family over the summer was going to be nearly impossible. And the problem was nobody would believe it anyway.

Mrs. Staller was asking for a 500-word story about our summer vacations, and while most kids would write about happy trips to Mt. Rushmore or riding record-setting roller coasters, I didn't even know where to start. Where could I? There was Art's floatplane dive-bombing me and the collapse of the lookout tower and where was I supposed to squeeze in the mysterious disappearance of Jimmy Longstockings?

I guess everything went back to Grandpa Tug. He was the one who taught me to count woodies and catch crawdads with my bare hands. Grandpa Tug's Bass Lake was a secret world where the sun felt so close it could only be tamed by the cool shade of towering Kentucky Coffee trees. It was a magical land of deep fried Twinkies, lawnmower races, and a world famous Fourth of July goat drop.

But everything changed when Grandpa left. Without him coming around, things grew so cold it felt like the whole earth had been jolted from its axis and was spiraling further and further from the warmth of the sun. For three long months my dad seemed lost in a fog, until he walked into my room one day and told me to pack up my stuff because we were going back to the lake. Almost immediately the sun came crashing through my window and filled my world again. This marked the beginning. The beginning of the Summer of Weird Harold.

Bass lake is three hours south of the city. Three hours from honking car horns, grumbling pedestrians, and El trains clacking down their tracks. I missed being at the lake so much that the three hours felt like three days.

I had my week planned out before we even got in the car. Looking for new birds in the swamp and swimming with the sunfish topped the list. I planned to fill in the gaps with a bunch of other stuff you could never do in the city.

"There's Harold," Mom groaned as we turned into the drive of our cottage. The Jeep's headlights cut through thick darkness before flashing across the ghostlike figure of our neighbor. His white bucket hat glowed in the dark. Slumped down in his chair, Harold Farcus looked like a spineless scarecrow that had collapsed into a heap of blue jeans and flannel.

His throne was a plastic lawn chair missing one leg. Here Harold sat, perched like a king, giving the stink eye to all who came and went along Lake Road.

"It's after midnight, why's he still sitting in his yard?" I asked.

"He was in that exact same spot when we left two years ago honey," Dad answered, sliding the gearshift into park. "I do think he changed shirts though." We paused to stare at the shadowy figure that was our neighbor.

"He's not moving," I said.

"Weird Harold's sure one creepy dude," shuddered my twin brother Kyle.

"Quit calling him weird. One of these days you're going to say that to his face and then what?" my dad asked.

"Then he'll know we think he's weird?" Kyle answered.

"Why's he always around? I mean he's always just sitting there staring at people and stuff. Why doesn't he just go inside and go to bed like any normal person would?"

"Harold's a lot like the weather, Sweetie," Mom answered quickly. "You never know what he's going to do next and you're just left to deal with it the best you can."

Rumor had it Farcus was a millionaire, though he wore nothing but faded blue jeans, ratty hunting flannels, and the same floppy bucket hat.

"I don't care what you say, Dad. That man is weird from head to toe."

"Cool it Kayla Marie."

"Why would anyone dress like a lumberjack in July? And up here of all places?" Kyle huffed.

My brother was right, things get so hot on Bass Lake in July that even lumberjacks would laugh at anyone dressed like a lumberjack there. Besides, you would think if Weird

Harold were a millionaire, he could at least look the part. Suit and tie, top hat and cane, fancy wing tip shoes; or at the very least, he could buy a chair with four legs.

Before I could ask if the reason Harold wasn't moving was because someone had superglued him to his chair, Mom handed Dad his marching orders. "I'll take the food in and put it away. You get the bags off the roof."

"What should we do?" Kyle asked.

"You should probably just stay in the car for the next two weeks," Dad answered quickly, "That's really the safest place for you."

"Mom? Is he serious?" Kyle whined.

"Your father is going to get out and talk to Harold. When he does, you two make a run for the cottage."

"Sounds like a game plan," Dad said.

An explosion of light filled the jeep when Dad threw his door open. "Hey there Harold!" he called out, tossing a friendly wave into the night.

There was no answer. An awkward moment was filled by crickets surging from the weeds. Maybe Weird Harold was ignoring my dad, or maybe he'd spontaneously combusted leaving only his blue jeans, hat, and flannel behind. Now that would be weird.

Dad went to work untying the bags on the roof as I glanced at Kyle. We were both thinking the same thing. Instead of running for the cottage, we wanted a closer look at Harold.

Careful not to wake our older sister, Kyle crawled over Abby as if he were the son of a navy seal or ninja instead of a deputy assistant to the mayor of Chicago. It was both an athletic and smart move on his part because Mom always said Abby was about as pleasant as a bag of rattlesnakes when she

Eric Walker Williams

first woke up. With weird Harold lingering just outside the door, the last thing we needed was a rhumba of rattlesnakes slithering around in the Jeep.

Abby was just a teenager, but most of the time she went around acting like the queen of some far away country. A place where people only care about hair products and finding the perfect outfit to match their eyes. It was a country Kyle and I had nicknamed Hormonestan and our sister was the unquestioned queen.

In the dim light Harold's chair was empty. He'd vanished faster than Houdini. "He was just sitting right there," I whispered to Kyle. "Now he's gone."

"Maybe he's like Sue Storm or something. You know, he's still sitting there but we just can't see him."

"Sue Storm?" I repeated.

"Yeah, Fantastic Four? The Invisible Woman?"

My brother Kyle is a total movie freak, and by 'freak' I don't mean he just loves watching movies. Watching movies is totally normal, and 'totally normal' and Kyle Minnix are four words that don't share space in the same sentence very often. In this case, 'freak' means no matter the situation, Kyle always finds something from a movie to match it.

As we were busy probing the darkness for signs of life, Harold's raspy voice emerged from the shadows next to our dad, "Sorry to hear about Tug, Wally. S'pose you'll be puttin' the place up for sale at the end of the year?"

"Gonna spend some time catching a few rays, Harold. That's all," Dad explained.

My dad seemed to answer Harold's question without really giving an answer, but there was no time to overthink things. The strap he was tugging soon broke loose, causing an avalanche of bags to come crashing down around him.

Grumbling loudly, he kicked hard at a suitcase. I was pretty sure I heard the same word Kyle shouted after striking out to lose the Cook County World Series. For that my brother had gotten his mouth washed out with soap; and I mean cursing, not losing the World Series.

"Things aren't the same up here anymore, Wally," Harold wheezed, offering no help with the bags.

From inside the Jeep, Kyle and I watched the man's dark figure shamble away. Dad said something about it feeling strange to be at the lake without Grandpa Tug, but there was no answer. Harold was gone.

"Dude's like a spy," Kyle muttered. "Here one minute, gone the next. Maybe Weird Harold's just a cover name or something. Farcus, Harold Farcus," he said in the deepest voice a twelve year old boy could possibly muster.

Kyle's theory sounded completely ridiculous. Still, something about it didn't seem all that farfetched. It was true nobody really knew what Harold did for a living. Nobody really knew where he got all his money either. And if he was a double agent, there appeared no better identity to fake than a recluse living in a ramshackle cabin on a tiny lake in the Midwest.

"I wonder if he has all the codes to our nukes? I'll bet they're written on the inside of that hat. Probably why he never takes it off!"

Before I could picture Harold in the war room launching nuclear warheads, or using uranium laced fishing lures to foil a Russian plot to dominate the world, a series of strange sounds emerged from behind his cottage. A loud banging. The shrill rattle of metal crashing to the ground. The unsettling shriek of a cat.

"What the heck's that weirdo doing back there?" I asked.

"Who cares?" Abby snarled. "Just get out of the way already, you little losers!" A well placed size seven forced Kyle and I out the door.

Her royal majesty was in rare form as she blasted out of the Jeep, stormed up the cottage steps and let herself inside like she owned the place. A 'hurricane of hormones' Grandpa Tug would say.

"Honey?" Mom asked from the front porch, "Why's my makeup bag running away?"

All eyes fell on mom's little black bag which was bouncing up the drive as if it had sprung legs. "Dang you, Tricky!" Dad howled.

All eyes were locked on the makeup bag as it was busy bolting away like a frightened squirrel crossing an interstate. Tricky? Was it that same troublemaking raccoon Grandpa Tug had spent so many years trying to outsmart? Before I could train my eyes on Tricky, that rascal had disappeared, paws clattering into the night.

"They're gettin' big money for property up here now days, Wally," Harold's voice returned, folding his frail body back into his three legged chair. The man's tone was steady and showed no concern for the fact a wild animal had just committed a serious crime, "Over on the other side of the lake they're rippin' out trees and puttin' up them high priced condos."

Building condos? On the lake? Weird Harold was finally speaking a language I understood. The far side of the lake was sacred ground, a place far too important for anyone to be building anything.

The swamp on the far side of the lake was where Grandpa Tug and I counted heron rookeries every spring. Perched high in the sycamore boughs, the last thing those fragile little eggs needed was a jackhammer in their front yard. Weird Harold sent a shiver up my spine, but thoughts of construction on the far side of the lake had my stomach tumbling.

"How's Jimmy doing?" Dad asked. "Been around much lately?"

"Change is inevitable, Wally. It's what you do with it that matters," Harold confessed, completely ignoring my dad's question as only a man whose nickname was 'weird' could. "But I'll *never* sell my cottage. They could wave a million dollar check in my face and I wouldn't bat an eye at it."

A million dollars? Suddenly all the things Weird Harold could buy with a million dollars flashed through my mind. Some new clothes, a hearing aid, maybe some classes on how to carry on a normal conversation. I watched Harold's shadowy figure rise from his chair. He seemed to float like a ghost to the edge of Lake Road where he stopped to stare out across the black water.

"Red sky at night, Larry," Harold declared. "No reason to hole up now, friend."

Larry? My mind ran down everyone in the immediate vicinity. There was only Mom and Dad, my brother Kyle, Tricky the make-up wearing raccoon and the Queen of Hormonestan. As far as I could tell, there were no Larrys to be found anywhere.

Tiny lights from distant cottages shimmered across the lake. A moment lingered as the chirping of crickets rose and fell sharply like someone pumping an accordion. I stood waiting for Larry's response as the sound of a fish splashed through the darkness.

An uncomfortable feeling began settling over me, so I headed for the cabin, leaving Harold and his imaginary friend alone outside. The cottage was just as I remembered. The same wood paneling on the walls and golden hardwood floors. The same faded curtains with the same outdoor print; bears and canoes and pine trees.

Above the couch hung the wooden sign with cursive letters burnt into it that read "Welcome to the Lake" and, in the corner closest to the fireplace, a pair of waders and Grandpa's bamboo fly rod sat waiting right where he had left them.

Grandma Minnie's rug was still there too, as was Kyle's grape juice stain. Grandpa Tug said if you looked at the stain just right you could see the state of Alaska, but Grandma Minnie hadn't been amused. I could still hear her howling around the cottage about my numbskull brother ruining a rug that had been in her family for three generations. That how somewhere her own grandmother was 'turning over in her grave'.

Grandpa Tug had been quick to point out, "It doesn't matter if your grandmother turns over in her grave Minnie, just means she wouldn't be able to see the stain anyway!"

Inside we went about unpacking our things. Kyle and I shared the front bedroom overlooking the lake. Abby had the larger room down the hall. Mom and Dad took Grandpa's old room downstairs.

"Kay?" Mom called up from the kitchen. "Be a dear and get my book from the car."

Sliding my flip flops on, I zipped downstairs and hurried out the front door. Mom's book was waiting on the passenger seat. But when I shut the door, something else was waiting for me too. It was Weird Harold Farcus, standing so close our shadows became one.

His face glowed green under the security light of the shed. He looked like something from another planet, or maybe a gangly man with a crooked nose and really bad teeth who'd fallen into vat of plutonium. My guess was too much time spent casting Russian fishing lures.

That's when I saw them. Small and round, like tiny black marbles, his eyes were perhaps best classified as belonging in the ferret family. "Better be careful up here sweetheart," he cautioned. "The lake can be a dangerous place." The word 'place' hissed from his mouth like a rattlesnake's warning. "I'd hate to see a little girl like you get hurt."

Tripping over my heel, I fell backwards into the gravel. Without speaking, I scrambled to my feet and raced for the cottage, leaving Harold alone in the drive. Standing in the doorway with my heart pounding, the sizzle of cicadas filled my ears. I peered out at Weird Harold one last time. He was staring across Lake Road toward the dark water.

Spotty moonlight through the coffee trees dotted his rangy figure, but the white bucket hat couldn't be missed. In thirty years of coming to the lake, Harold Farcus had never once spoken to my family. Now he was asking questions and full of advice.

Grandpa Tug told stories about strange things on the lake. Boats sinking, barefoot skiing squirrels, catfish so large they could swallow the bait, the hook, and a toddler too. And of course the Great Muskrat Scourge of '88. A time when so many of those slippery little rodent devils were lurking about that people didn't dare dip a toe in the water for fear it be nibbled off. But nothing, nothing topped Harold Farcus. He was 100% Grade A Weird.

Outside my window the moon crept over the lake. Down by the water a lonely bullfrog drummed loudly. As troubling as it was to hear someone was building condos on the lake, my mind couldn't shake Weird Harold. When I closed my eyes, I saw the peculiar way his ferret-like eyes hid beneath that white bucket hat. I could see his rail thin frame and rattletrap cottage. I could hear his raspy voice choking out the warning, 'The lake can be a dangerous place'.

That's when I turned to the one person who'd looked after me for so long. The one person I trusted more than any on Earth. It was at that moment I asked Grandpa Tug to protect me from Weird Harold Farcus.

2

~~~~~~

When the sun rises on Bass Lake, a flurry of boaters take to the water. Fishermen curse ski boats while the skiers are busy swatting wave runners away like mosquitoes. With these noises of the lake buzzing around me, I pointed my bike down our driveway.

Peering out across the water, the silver maples winked back at me. They were fellow guardians of the swamp, a magical place Grandpa Tug and I had always looked after. The swamp on the far side of the lake was the place where deer came down to nibble on clover and red heads drum on the elms.

For three years straight my brother Kyle had asked for a trip to Disney World for Christmas, but for me, wading through the goldenrod and hemlock to find a red-eared slider sunning himself was the only real magic kingdom that existed. Returning to the swamp was at the top of my list of things to do at the lake, so I pedaled my bike out onto Lake Road.

Harold's cottage was the first thing I saw. His property was littered with Keep Out signs. There must have been two dozen of them. They were tacked to the trees, tacked to the fence, one hung beside the front door and another on the mailbox. There was even a large one in the front window.

Eric Walker Williams

I'd never noticed Harold's window before. It had no curtains and was filled with a single craggy tree limb. A silvery stuffed opossum clung to the limb, his tiny pink nose pointed at the lake. Looking at his yard and all the warning signs, I wondered if those who didn't keep out found themselves stuffed. Either way, it would be hard to argue Harold was anything but weird.

"Didn't you think it was really strange the way Harold kept disappearing last night?" I asked Kyle.

"I thought it was weird the way Dad was asking him questions about stuff and Harold kept talking about other stuff."

"Really? Because you're the king of that."

"What are you talking about?" Kyle huffed.

"Remember when Mrs. McDonald was grilling you about quadratic equations? Don't act like you forgot what you said."

"I know what I said. I told her how to work a quadratic equation."

"No. I'm pretty sure everyone clearly heard you tell our math teacher the yellowhammer was the state bird of Alabama. Which, I never told you, was actually quite impressive."

"I think I heard you say it one time at breakfast or something."

The July heat rose around me. My tires made a funny squishing sound against the road, as if at any moment they might change their minds and turn to liquid. Lake Road was firecracker hot.

"Where are we going again?" Kyle asked, struggling to pedal Dad's oversized bike.

"The swamp."

"And why are we going to the swamp again?"

"I told you, I haven't been there for two years. Nobody's been there for two years. I need to make sure everything is still where we left it."

"Right…it's just that it's so far away. I mean, can't we just ask Dad to drive us over there or something?"

Ahead a finch rose and fell, bobbing toward cover. From the ditch, stalks of goldenrod swayed in a soft breeze. A patch of foxglove rolled by, bumblebees bobbing in and out of the white bonnets. Rounding the bend quickly, I spotted the tops of the silver maples getting closer.

"Come on, we're almost there!"

Grandpa Tug's swamp log was in my backpack. Fifty years of notes and bird counts I planned to add to. In fact, I wanted to do more than just add to them. I was out to find the crown jewel of swamp birds. The one that had eluded my grandpa for all these years. I planned to find the glossy ibis.

My dad said I could never learn the Latin names of every state bird in the United States but, by the start of second grade, I had. When I put my mind to something, I find a way to get it done. Mom says I'm hard headed, but I prefer the label determined, and that first day back in the swamp I had channeled all my determination toward one goal, finding a glossy ibis.

At the swamp we ditched our bikes along the road. A pair of zebra swallowtails floating over a patch of yellow sorrel greeted us. This was it. I was home. It had been a long two years away. Two years of trying to convince my parents I'd seen every bird that called Lincoln Park home. Two years of trying to make sense of all the changes. Two years of trying to get myself back to this place. Right here, right now.

"So, what do we do now?" Kyle asked.

I kicked him in the shin. "You have to be quiet!" I barked in a whisper. "We won't see anything if you're going to walk around talking to me like that."

Kyle stopped to rub his leg as I pressed on. The prickle weeds scratched at me as I edged toward the sweet murky water. Sliding Grandpa's swamp log from the bag, I kept my ears open for the soft bleating of the ibis. This was the kind of place they would love. The perfect spot. Shallow water, thick reeds, plenty of small prey to gobble down.

Nothing had changed about the swamp. Life was thriving beneath a canopy of black willow and maple trees. A thick cluster of arrowhead plants came into focus. Grandpa Tug called them the 'duck potato', even though you were more likely to find a beaver or muskrat eating them. Just beyond the arrowheads lay Mentone's oak. Resting where it had fallen over a hundred years before, that old oak may have been dead, but it was still home to dozens of creatures.

"Hold still Kay," Kyle suggested.

He was panning around the swamp with the digital video camera Mom and Dad had given him for Christmas.

"What are you doing?"

"Hey, while I'm here, I might as well shoot some footage. This might make a good opening scene for my movie."

"You're making a movie about the swamp?"

"No, I'm making a movie about the lake. It's going to be a docudrama about a family vacation. I'm going to fill it with drama, suspense and danger."

"Sounds great, but there's nothing suspenseful or dangerous about the lake, Kyle. In fact you couldn't have picked a worse place to find any of that stuff."

"That's the magic of filmmaking. It's up to me to take the ordinary and bring out suspense and danger."

"Okay. Good luck with that."

I didn't have time for my brother's Hollywood fantasies. I had work to do. My pulse surged with the thought of finding an ibis. That's when an entirely different sound filled the swamp. Low and steady, it was a song unlike any I'd heard before.

Rattling, rambling and entirely off key, the noise filled my ears. "Met Mr. Catfish comin' down stream, says Mr. Catfish, what does you mean? Caught Mr. Catfish by the snout, and turned Mr. Catfish wrong side out."

The singing fell into a soft hum. Pushing aside a hemlock bough, I found we weren't alone in the swamp. Skirting the edge of the water was an older woman. She was a stick figure in bright pink shorts and oversized floppy sun hat; the brim of which was pinned back to clear her vision. Her nose was pasted with sun block and her eyes hid beneath oversized black sunglasses that wrapped around her face making her look like an alien.

I put my free hand over Kyle's mouth. Using a marshmallow roasting stick, the woman was busy jabbing at stray pieces of litter. In her other hand she clutched a paper bag large enough to carry my brother in.

"Why hello there!" she beamed, stabbing a Styrofoam cup like a heron spearing a fish.

I didn't know what to do. I'd never seen another person in the swamp before. This swamp belonged to Grandpa Tug and me. Sure, we'd never put any signs up, but we clearly owned it. After all, we were the only ones who took care of it. The only ones who ever dropped by and took bird counts or made sure the nesting boxes were cleaned out at the end of the year.

And now someone else was in the swamp. Our swamp. What was I supposed to do now? Kyle would probably tell me to just pretend I was Sue Storm and turn myself invisible, but that seemed a fruitless move. She had waved after all. But what could I do? Acting like the daughter of a caveman who spoke in only grunts and gestures seemed a stretch as well.

Still if I was going to find a glossy ibis, this woman had to stop talking. The ibis can be skittish, and all this singing and humming and conversation would be enough to scare one back onto its nest for a month.

"My name's Agnes, and you?"

My response was to release the hemlock bough only to have it flip back and smack me in the face, almost knocking me over. Pain tore over my face before racing to my brain, where it met the part of me that wanted to say letting go of the branch before moving my face had been a really bad idea.

"Well come on now, you don't have to hide back there."

I fell to one knee, rubbing my face with both hands. This meant Kyle's mouth was no longer covered. "My name's Kyle Minnix. This is my sister Kayla," he seemed to shout.

I stood up quickly and kicked him again, "I told you to whisper!" With one hand cradling his camera, he rubbed his leg with the other.

"Why are we whispering dear?" Agnes asked, stepping over the clumps of bur-reed and jewelbox to reach me.

I wanted so badly to tell this woman I wouldn't find my ibis unless she left the swamp immediately, and by immediately, I meant run away like her hair was on fire.

Agnes was long and thin. Her skin was tanned like leather, wrinkly and littered with sunspots. Her golden blonde hair was stringy and floated on the heat, waving up and down like the arms of a ghost. A pair of dainty wrists disappeared into oversized orange gardeners' gloves. Like roads on a map, dark veins wandered around her legs as if she had no exterior layer of skin. Just below the knee, Agnes' puny calves disappeared in a pair of rubber storm boots.

"What are you doing here?" I finally asked.

"Well, I'm trying to clean this place up. Look at it dearie. It's just a hot mess around here."

"But that thing's for roasting hot dogs and marshmallows," Kyle observed.

"This?" Agnes said, holding the roasting fork up, "Why, I call this my double barrel. I can get two pieces at once with this baby. Stuff blows in from the road all the time. People can be so careless." She drew in a deep breath while casting a hopeless look around the swamp, "Besides, somebody's gotta take care of this place. Otherwise it'll be gone someday."

Agnes clearly had no idea who she was talking to. Grandpa Tug and I had taken care of this place since forever. In fact we'd been doing so long before Agnes and her roasting stick and songs about catfish had ever stumbled into the swamp.

Agnes didn't belong here. Sure we hadn't gone all Weird Harold on the swamp and tacked a Keep Out sign to every tree, but clearly this was no place for other people. This place was for Grandpa Tug and me.

"And what brings you two out here today?" she asked.

"Well, I'm filming a docudrama called the *Curse of Bass Lake* and my sister's looking for birds."

I felt Grandpa Tug's book under my arm. Fifty years of work or more condensed to 100 pages. I'd read through his notes and bird counts dozens of times and had found a grand total of zero references to a Trash Queen named Agnes.

"A birder! Well, can't say as I've seen too much this morning." Agnes admitted while dragging the back of her wrist across her nose. "Scared a few great blues and a pair of red- winged blackbirds up on my way in, but I s'pose, with a book like that, you're looking for big game. Am I right dearie?"

I didn't know what to say. For the first time in my life there were no words in my brain so I just stood there, staring at the Trash Queen as if I'd been born without a tongue.

"Well? What is it? Wood thrush? Grasshopper sparrow? You looking for woodcock? Because I'm afraid it's far too late in the day for that."

"Ibis, glossy ibis," I choked out meekly.

"Glossy ibis!" Agnes cackled, "Good luck with that, sweetheart. The ibis doesn't come around here very much. They prefer life on the coast. I'm afraid finding one out here would be nothing more than a stroke of luck!"

I wasn't about to let the Trash Queen know this, but she wasn't telling me anything I didn't already understand. Birders knew the ibis as a casual visitor to the swamp, but still Grandpa and I had heard them here before. We'd also seen marks in the mud where they'd been using their sickle shaped bills to probe for insects.

Actually, if Agnes wanted to know, my best hope was to find a pair nesting with the herons because the ibis is known to do this occasionally. "My grandpa and I have heard them here before," I explained, trying hard to hide how annoyed I was. "Mostly singles, ones that probably wandered away from the colony. Tends to happen with them quite a bit."

A surprised look spread over the Trash Queen's face. "Well, a glossy ibis is a tall order to fill little missy, but you look up to it," She declared with a wink. "What about that book of yours? What kinds of things do you have in there?"

The log was none of the Trash Queen's business. It was off limits to outsiders. It was a world nobody else would understand. "Just some stuff," I answered shortly, trying to dismiss the importance of the book.

But calling it 'just some stuff' was like saying the famous birder John James Audubon could draw 'pretty well'. The log was clearly more than just 'some stuff'. It was a life's work. It was every note my grandpa had ever made, every sketch, every observation and every count he'd ever done. It was far more than just 'some stuff'. It was an entire history of the most magical place on the face of the earth.

"What kind of stuff, dearie?"

My head was swirling as I tried to answer. I didn't know what to say. I didn't want her to see the book. The swamp log wasn't for outsiders and the Trash Queen wasn't welcome in our world.

"Birds mostly, it's just mostly about birds," I stammered. "You know, bird stuff…about birds…and stuff."

I kept my arm locked tightly on Grandpa's book, hoping my interrogation was soon to be over. Agnes looked at me as if I had three eyes. She laid her double barrel against an elm tree while racking her oversized sunglasses on her head. I watched her slip a wrinkly hand from her glove before extending it toward the book.

"Do you mind?" she asked.

Seeing the Trash Queen's eyes for the first time made her face take on a new expression. She seemed warm and harmless. There was something almost familiar in Agnes now. Something in her steely blue eyes said I could trust this total stranger, some strange power that made me hand the log over.

Eric Walker Williams

She took it in her hands, cradling it like an archaeologist might an Egyptian artifact. "This is incredible," she said softly, leafing through the pages. "Why, it goes all the way back to the Seventies!"

"It belongs to my Grandpa Tug. He's the one who wrote everything down."

"I see that, but I also see your name a bunch too. It says here 'Kayla spotted a yellow breasted chat on her own today'. Well, I guess you're quite the little birder now aren't you? Don't s'pose you need me telling you about the ibis."

Her face lit up with each page turned. It was clear Agnes the Trash Queen appreciated what she was reading.

"Well, this is a real treasure you've got here young Kayla. Your grandpa sounds like an incredible man."

She carefully shut the book with her wrinkly hands before handing it back to me. "I've seen a pair of wood thrush and a little green heron nosing around in here before, but I'm afraid there's been no glossy ibis."

The Trash Queen reached down and picked a small piece of plastic off the swamp floor before tossing it into her bag. Jammed with plastic wrappers and Styrofoam cups, the bag was bulging like something that belonged best on Santa's sleigh. If Santa was a garbage man who flew around the world shoving unwanted junk under people's Christmas trees. There were cigarette boxes and coffee stained auction flyers, empty French fry containers and wadded up burger wrappers. A haze of flies and gnats were milling around the opening.

"Well, I'll leave you two alone so you can complete your mission," the Trash Queen said, beaming widely. "Good luck finding your ibis!"

She picked up her double barrel and bag before turning to walk away. As she left, her voice started back up, lower and softer than before, "Came to a river and I couldn't get across. Paid five dollars for an old blind hoss…"

I let Grandpa's book fall open to a random page. There was a sketch of a flicker, all its various colors labeled. Beneath the sketch was a hand written note. His letters were so precise. I'd never noticed them before. They were so uniform and perfect, as if punched out with a typewriter. They read: "The flicker has so many colors, Kayla called it a 'clown bird'."

That day was fuzzy in my brain. So many things had changed since we saw that flicker, but not the swamp. The swamp was like a perfectly preserved world. Suspended magically in time, the swamp didn't know change. It had been this way for millions of years.

From the jewelweed to the sorrel to the sweet smelling muck, nothing had changed since the last time Grandpa Tug and I had been here. It was almost as if he'd placed it in a Ziplock bag and left it in the fridge for me to open up and enjoy later.

Unfortunately, change was coming to the swamp. It wouldn't be something small like finding the Trash Queen wandering through it. Big changes were coming. In fact, at that very moment a tidal wave of change was barreling down on the one place I loved more than any other on earth.

Eric Walker Williams

3

~~~~~~~

Most days the lake is like a magnet, pulling you down to the water. When we returned from the swamp, Kyle fell under the magnet's spell and wanted to go swimming. The morning sun was growing warmer as I stood along shore wiggling my toes in the grass. Three red jet skis raced across the water in a perfect V formation. I imagined them a gaggle of geese in flight. In a carnival of sound, the thunder of the boats and shrieks of children being pulled on tubes echoed over the water.

Every part of me believed I'd find Grandpa Tug waiting at the end of the pier. That's where he always was first thing in the morning, staring out at the lake, blowing steam from his coffee. But now the bench sat empty. The wood was faded and the boards squeaked under my feet. The arms of grandpa's bench felt rough and warped. He had built it himself, but now it looked like an ancient relic, something that belonged best inside a museum case.

Grandpa was famous for his smiles and knew a million punch lines. He had the heart of a lion and I thought about him every day. But now there was no roaring laughter or corny jokes to greet me, just the whine of a distant jet ski. Standing there with the world moving forward, I could see him looking up from the water, winking back while saying, "Sure thing, Jitterbug. Whatever you want."

Dad said we'd come back to the lake to 'sort things out', whatever that meant. Abby said it meant finding somebody to buy the cottage, but Kyle and I didn't believe that. Besides, I knew the real reason we'd come back was because Grandpa hadn't been to the lake for a while, so Mom and Dad needed to check on things.

Either way, I was back at the lake, and things were going to be the way they always were. I wanted to swim all day and roast marshmallows at night. I wanted to watch mother ducks training their young and listen for screech owls calling after dark.

"Watch this, Kay!" My brother wailed while running down the pier. He tried to dive, but his feet went up over his head, and he flopped awkwardly into the water. He looked like a frozen fish somebody had tossed from a boat. I said he was athletic; I didn't say he was graceful.

Not to be outdone, I sprang to my feet and bolted to the end of the pier before launching myself into the water. The chill stung my skin, but somehow it felt perfect. When I came up, Kyle was doing a handstand, his skinny legs flailing in the air. The morning sun warmed my neck as I stood still, swirling my foot on the sandy bottom, pretending it was a walking catfish.

Kyle splashed his way to the surface. "Dad says he's getting Grandpa's Toy out. Are you going to ski?" he asked.

"I don't think so," I answered quickly.

If there was only one thing Grandpa Tug loved more than birding in the swamp, it was skiing. I'd never been able to learn, and it had left a hole in me. Grandpa wanted so badly for me to learn, I just couldn't. I had tried and tried and tried, so much so blisters had formed on my hands.

Still, I just couldn't. The skis were so big and so awkward. They moved around all over the place and made you feel like you were trying to stand on ice, but Grandpa never got mad once. He just kept saying, "Keep at it kid! It'll come. Don't you quit on me!"

"What about riding in town and trying to find the hot dog guy instead?" Kyle asked.

"Eww, hot dogs? Seriously? No thanks. Do yourself a favor and never look up what they actually put inside those things."

"Whatever. Hey! Watch this! Water cartwheel!" Kyle announced, twisting his body into another handstand. I watched as he tried to cartwheel only to fall backwards into the water again.

For a moment it felt like it always had. A bright summer sun overhead, the lush green lawn tucked up against the cottage. The cool water and soft lake bottom, an endless powder blue sky above.

And then there was Harold, watching it all from inside his redwood fence. He was moving around his yard, straightening the Keep Out signs. Under the arm of his flannel coat he was carrying a small white animal with him. I didn't remember Harold having a dog, but whenever he wasn't moving a sign back in place, he was sure to stroke the animal's head with a caring hand.

His warning from the night before echoed in my head. The way he'd called the lake a dangerous place. I'm not sure why it bothered me so much. To me, nothing was further from the truth. Bass Lake was an amazing place. One where there was absolutely nothing to be afraid of.

As I stood wondering about this strange man and his run at the Guinness record for Keep Out signs, a dark shadow passed overhead. A black spot so large it seemed to blot the sun. "Hey, check out the plane!" Kyle yelled, pointing toward the sky with wide eyes.

My brother's face didn't say 'plane', it screamed 'UFO!' or 'Santa's sleigh!' We watched the plane fish hook around the far end of the lake. Sputtering along, it swayed awkwardly like an eaglet leaving its nest for the first time. That's when it started flying lower.

"Why's he flying so low?" I asked, stepping back nervously.

As it buzzed closer, the ballasts bolted to the wings came into sharp focus. This was no ordinary airplane; this was a floatplane. But what was a floatplane doing at the lake? Sure there were plenty of boats, a few canoes and one or two kayaks. But a plane? Nobody with half a brain would ever think of landing a plane on tiny Bass Lake.

"He's heading right for us!" I warned.

"I know! This is totally cool!!!" Kyle shrieked. The words 'totally cool' came out of my brother's mouth like a little girl seeing her first doll house. Boats, jet skis, and windsurfers scrambled for an escape. Like an inchworm crossing a super-highway, a helpless Boy Scout paddled hard to get his canoe out of the way.

With eager eyes, my brother watched the floats touch down in the water. The plane bounced closer as the once distant whine of the engine soon swelled to an ear-splitting roar.

That was the moment it happened. The moment I froze. This monstrous plane was clearly heading straight for me, and yet I couldn't move. I wanted very much to dive out of the way, to swim for shore or run for the pier, but I

Eric Walker Williams

couldn't. Shock had wrapped me up like a wet towel, and now my body and mind were absorbed in an argument at the worst possible moment.

This was nothing new. My body and mind had a history of getting into it. The first time had been during gym class, as I stood staring down a speeding dodge ball. This wasn't just any speeding dodge ball, mind you. This speeding dodge ball had come from the hand of Roni Bonafetti. Perhaps you've heard of her. She is after all a world class dodge ball hurler. Her dad's a professional softball coach and part time steel worker, and Roni has the right arm of an Olympic weightlifter. I got a black eye that day, and it wasn't until seventh period, when I aced a science test that Roni clearly had not, that all seemed right with the world again.

But this plane wasn't your run of the mill speeding dodgeball. The roaring engine, the propeller whirling like a giant buzz saw. Before I could even think of screaming, it was on top of me. The plane was moments away from ending my all too short life, when the propeller seemed to sprout a face. A large pair of menacing eyes glowered at me while it's giant, gaping mouth looked ready to swallow me whole.

It couldn't end this way. I was closing in on my thirteenth birthday and still had so many plans. That moment something took control of me, something told me to react. Maybe it was instinct, maybe it was luck, or maybe it was Grandpa Tug not wanting to see his Jitterbug get hurt. Whatever it was, as I stood microseconds from being diced into human confetti by an airplane that was clearly 10,000 times too large for tiny Bass Lake, something told me to dive for the bottom. And I did, a split second before the shadow of the floats raced overhead like a pair of torpedoes missing their mark.

The force of the churning water sent me tumbling. When I rose to the surface whitecaps were washing ashore, as a tornado of dirt and loose grass swirled about. Kyle stood, hypnotized from head to toe. The expression on his face was all boy, awed by the thundering dinosaur with wings docking itself next door.

"That thing is amazing!" He gushed. "It looks just like the one Indiana Jones used to escape that angry tribe of dart-shooting Peruvians in *Raiders of the Lost Ark*!"

My heart was pounding like a jackhammer. I didn't have time for more of my brother's movie nonsense. That pilot had just landed his plane as if there were *nobody* else on the lake. Not to mention he'd come inches away from running me over without so much as a courteous honk of the horn or 'Sorry! Didn't see you there!'

"I think the one used in the film was a Waco Bi-Plane, so it's not exactly the same," Kyle explained as if anyone really cared at that exact moment. "Doesn't change the fact that it's absolutely incredible that a floatplane just landed right in front of me! And you know what else? Now, I've got some adventure for my movie!"

"Kyle, do you realize how close he came to hitting me?"

The question snapped my brother's focus, "Uh, no. Are you okay?"

"I could have been flattened by that maniac and all you care about is determining the model of some dumb airplane from some stupid movie?"

"Sorry, sis. I guess I got carried away. It's just that it's not every day a float plane lands in front of you and docks itself next door."

The plane's obnoxious roar soon sputtered, ending with a combustion fueled belch. We stood waiting for an apology, as the spinning of the propeller slowly came to a stop. The lake's orchestra of rumbling ski boats and whining jet skis resumed, breaking up the sudden silence.

The cockpit windows were tinted black. The words 'Big A's Real Estate' had been scribbled down the fuselage in cursive red letters. The pilot's door swung open, and a large rakish man jumped out. He wore a loud Bermuda print shirt and leather sandals.

The pilot grabbed a rope and pulled the giant winged beast closer to shore with such ease, he made the plane look like a plastic bathtub toy.

Before I could tell this Sasquatch in sandals what I thought about his thundering dinosaur with wings, more people spilled out. A beautiful woman, bright sunlight glinting off a string of diamonds around her neck. She was followed by two children. A boy with spiked hair and a girl with a perfect ponytail and shades so dark you'd think she was a Hollywood starlet. They looked like the typical snotty-faced kids whose parents would own an airplane.

As the group headed for shore, the pilot flipped open the luggage bin in the tail of the plane. Pulling out a long white tube, he tucked it under his arm before heading up the pier.

"Look at that airplane, Kyle!" Dad said, crossing the road to join us.

He'd been behind the cottage fiddling with something in the shed. Of course, this meant he had no idea how close his children had come to being mowed down by an airplane. Clearly, it had not been a father-of-the-year moment.

"The Big A's here," I answered sarcastically.

"The Big A?" he repeated.

"The Big A..." Kyle responded, still somewhat breathless. He spoke the man's name as if he knew exactly who the

'Big A' was and longed with every fiber of his being to be just like him someday. I felt like yakking.

I mean, just because you have enough money to buy an airplane and pay someone to tattoo your name down the side of it, does that mean everyone should automatically know who you are? Besides that, could somebody really be so important they needed their name painted on the side of a plane anyway? My dad worked for the Mayor of Chicago, but that didn't mean he felt the need to sharpie his name on the door of our Jeep.

I looked back at the airplane people milling around in front of the cottage next door. They looked confused, almost like cows put out to graze in a parking lot. This made sense, because they weren't Bass Lake people after all. They, and their plane, didn't belong in Grandpa Tug's world. Maybe they would fit in some place like Alaska, where the bush people have to fly their groceries in, or Hawaii, where the locals hop from island to island to visit friends. But not here. Not on Bass Lake.

Something in the pit of my stomach was saying we'd be better off leaving at that moment. A tiny voice whispering the words, 'get out of here now'. My eyes wandered over to Harold in his lawn chair, sitting inside that struggling redwood fence of his in grass up to his knees. As creepy as he was, the look peering out from under the brim of that bucket hat was clear. He wasn't impressed by the airplane either.

Eric Walker Williams

4

~~~~~~~

In the fading light a pair of swallows flirted with an evening swim. Diving in acrobatic circles, their tiny wings were a blur. We were supposed to be enjoying a barbecue courtesy of our new neighbors, but for obvious reasons that was proving difficult. I tried to keep busy watching the swallows, wanting to make it clear I hadn't appreciated our lopsided game of chicken earlier in the day. That, and the fact swallows are really cool.

The Big A said his real name was Art Guilafante. While he was making all nice with my parents, he was yet to apologize for almost shredding Kyle and me. Weird Harold Farcus had not been invited, but that didn't mean he wasn't interested. It was hard to miss him, standing motionless at the shore like a statue celebrating weirdness. Only this time he wasn't alone, for at his feet sat a small animal in a coat of white streaked with gray, peering out at the lake just like his master. Harold clutched a short leash in his hand, his eyes peeled toward the water.

"I didn't know Harold had a dog," Abby said, causing all eyes to swivel in the man's direction.

"Looks like a Pom-Pom," Art said, as if he were suddenly a judge for the Westminster Kennel Club instead of a kamikaze pilot of an obnoxiously large float plane.

"I don't think it has enough hair to be a Pom-Pom, Art," my mom added.

"Maybe he shaves it. Shaving a dog sounds like something Weird Harold would do," Abby offered, doing her best to suck up to the millionaires next door.

"Weird Harold?" Art chuckled, shifting some burgers around on his grill. "Why do you call him that?"

"Well, everyone knows…" Abby started only to be cut off by my dad in the way only a dad could. "You know Art, that does look like a Pom-Pom. I think you're right."

As everyone was busy trying to identify Harold's dog, my eyes found his picture window. The craggy limb was still there, but the opossum was not.

"That dog hasn't moved at all," Art's wife Betsy announced. "I've been watching him for almost ten minutes, and he hasn't moved once."

"Must be very well trained," Art's daughter said, adjusting her way-too-fancy sunglasses.

"If I were standing next to Harold, I wouldn't move either," Kyle admitted, taking a break from drooling over Art's nearby floatplane.

Or maybe he hadn't moved because it wasn't a dog at all. Apparently Harold was taking his stuffed opossum for a walk. I could see the tail now. Rat-like in appearance, it had all the markings of an opossum's prehensile tail.

"That's some place he's got there," Art snorted, "Talk about a junk pile."

"Nothing a fresh coat of paint and a lawnmower wouldn't fix," My dad countered.

Eric Walker Williams

Before I could reveal my theory that our neighbor was in fact exercising a lifeless animal, Art started back up. "Really? I was thinking more like a bulldozer and a wrecking ball," he suggested with a thunderous laugh.

Part of me agreed with Art, though I would never admit it. Harold's cottage was a disaster. The roofline sagged, the paint was peeling, even the front porch looked tired, as if it could give up and collapse at any moment. An old wooden ski and a "KEEP OUT" sign had been hung with care over the front door. The ski looked so frail and dated it seemed a real possibility Abe Lincoln himself might have ridden it at one point.

It didn't help that Weird Harold's front yard was a jungle of uncut grass and head-high horseweeds. Everyone on the lake grumbled about the way Harold grew tomatoes in his front yard. Still, there they were, planted in a small patch between the miniature Dutch windmill and a concrete statue of the Virgin Mary bleached bone white from the sun.

"I think his cottage looks pretty nice," I said, just to tick Art off.

Art shot me a look. I could tell what he was thinking. He knew I was a handful. 'Prickly as a cactus and quick as a wink', Grandpa Tug would say.

It was no secret where the Big A got his nickname. Everything about the man was big.

Every bit of six foot seven, his big frame was carried around by two big feet that hung over what I could only guess to be size 38 sandals. His neck was thick and round like the trunk of a redwood tree, and a faint layer of buzzed hair covered the top of his big, watermelon-like head. Imagine Sasquatch with much less hair, designer sunglasses and a pilot's license, and you'd have Art Guilafante's twin.

"Hope we didn't scare the kids there too much earlier," Art finally apologized while flipping a burger over. "I've only been flying a few months and landings can still be tricky. They're all about the approach and the conditions, but I'm sure you don't need me telling you that."

He finished by shooting my parents a smile wearing a wink. I couldn't tell if this was a 'sorry I almost killed your children' wink or an 'I don't really mean anything I say' wink.

"Yeah, Dad's landings are terrible," Art's son added. The tone of his voice revealed Russell Guilafante's belief that every dad in the world knew how to fly an airplane.

"What about Jimmy? I didn't know he was looking to sell his cottage," my dad asked Art.

"The Strabobbis wanted to relocate. Florida, I think."

"Strabobbi?" Abby repeated somewhat confused. "His name was Jimmy Longstockings."

"Longstockings is a nickname," Kyle explained sharply.

In Hormonestan, a place where most laws involve the proper care and use of curling irons and *Teen Girl* the magazine is required reading in all schools, Jimmy Longstockings didn't have a real name. All these years my sister had imagined the man signing his Christmas cards:

Happy Holidays–Jimmy Longstockings.

"Grandpa called him longstockings because that was all he ever wore," Kyle explained, speaking in a tone that seemed both clear and insulting at the same time, "Remember? Long black dress socks with khaki shorts? Dress socks with cut-off jeans? And dress socks with that stars and stripes Speedo he always wore on the Fourth?"

Eric Walker Williams

No matter the occasion it seemed Jimmy Longstockings had a pair of long black dress socks to match it. And unless you happen live in a place like Wooloomooloo, Australia, everybody knows wearing long black dress socks and shorts together is not socially acceptable.

"But that cottage had been in his family for four generations!!" Dad said in shock.

"You know what they say, Walt, *everything* has a price tag," the Big A explained, offering another custom-made, cheese filled wink.

My dad hated being called Walt. Of course Art didn't know this, but the Big A seemed like the type who, even if he did know, wouldn't really care anyway. Forget the sun, Art's world revolved around Art Guilafante.

Taryn Guilafante didn't seem like she had strayed far from her father's shadow. She hid behind her way-too-fancy sunglasses, picking at her potato salad with a plastic fork as if eating it were somehow beneath her. Her brother Russell just kept talking about the jet-ski his dad had promised to buy, something about "Making sick chop until he burns the toast." At one point I wasn't even really sure he was still speaking English.

When the hamburgers were all done and Betsy Guilafante had trucked out a second pot of sweet corn, the Big A told us his company was the one buying up land on the far side of the lake to make room for condos. "This lake's got a lot of potential," he announced, leaning forward for some potato salad. Part of me fully expected his weight to upend the table and send all the plates rocketing to the far side of the lake.

His eyes flickered as he continued. "I see a really bright future here, Walt. It's kind of a sleepy little ghost town right now, charming in some respects, but also completely out-dated and backwards… but when we're done with her," Art paused to savor a devilish grin, "boy, you'll have a real first class tourist destination on your hands then, Walt."

"It's always been more of a family lake." My dad suggested weakly.

My heart fluttered. Was my dad trying to argue with the Big A? A small part of me felt so proud because Walter Minnix was not a confrontational person. Part of his job was to sit in a chair and let the Mayor of Chicago yell at him when things went wrong. When I told him to fight back, he would always say, "Fighting back means losing my job."

"Nothing stays the same anymore, Walt, everything's got a price tag," the Big A declared.

With Art blathering on about his vision of progress, a wrecking ball meeting a row of heron rookeries flashed through my mind. I saw helpless killdeer scurrying out from under the monstrous tires of an earthmover churning down the beach, and felt myself swelling up like a balloon.

I gnashed my teeth over the far side of the lake being torn up. Someone had to do something. Someone had to speak up for the shorebirds. I looked at Dad. He was dragging a potato chip through some dip. Clearly, his protest had gone about as far as he planned to take it.

"One condo brings in more money in a week than an entire row of cottages could turn over in a summer," Art added. "Its basic economics, but what will make this place really pop is a championship golf course and world class spa."

The words championship golf course and world class spa stuck me like a needle. That's when everything I was fighting back came gushing out, "What about the shorebirds? Last I checked, they don't golf."

Dad crunched a chip so loudly it seemed to echo across the lake. My sister's jaw dropped as Mom dropped a giant bowl of macaroni salad into Betsy Guilafante's lap.

"Oh Betsy! I'm so sorry!" My mom shrieked. Using her bare hands, she began raking the salad off the woman's lap and back into the bowl.

"Don't worry about it," Betsy Guilafante said, failing to hide the annoyed expression that had conquered her face. "This was an old outfit anyway. Would you please excuse me while I go inside and change?"

"Of course," Mom said, cranking her head toward me. At that moment, words were not necessary.

"Kayla, what happens on the far side of the lake is of no concern to you. Now, please, you're being rude to our hosts," my dad said, as if reading word for word from an 'Idiot's Guide to being a Responsible Parent'.

"Anyway, wait till you see what all these changes will do to your property values, Walt." Art Guilafante finished tossing my dad another disgusting wink.

He did so as if he and my father were both members of some exclusive club. One where men get together to play croquet and compare sports cars. One where they wear the same jackets, smoke long cigars and complain about hurricanes damaging their vacation homes.

Art went on gabbling about lakeside developments, the Swedish spa, world class golf course and row upon row of condominiums he would leave behind.

"Right now our golf course is only nine holes. It butts up against this godforsaken, bug infested swamp…"

Hearing the words 'bug infested swamp' caused the world around me to stop. In a muffled voice I heard Art saying something about draining the swamp and having the course ready for next season and how they'll get it done, they always do. His big, ugly face was frozen. My parents were saying something, but their voices came out as garbled nonsense.

Art Guilafante wanted to drain the swamp, the same swamp Grandpa Tug had taught me to love. The same swamp that hadn't changed since the dawn of time. Archaeologists had found fossils of the same sensitive fern plants that still grew on the floor of the swamp, and yet one jack-wagon comes down from Chicago with some big plans, and that's all it took to erase a million years' worth of natural beauty.

I steeled my blue eyes into slits. I wanted to see the swamp drained about as bad as a hog wants to see a shower stall and perfumed shampoo. I felt a strange knot tighten in my stomach. Grandpa Tug had taught me all about the wild-life around the lake. Important stuff like how the yellow billed cuckoo is known as a 'rain crow' because his call can mean a storm is coming. Or how the belted kingfisher beats its prey against a tree limb before feeding it to its young. My neck got hot watching Art shoving the last of his cheeseburger into his greedy mouth. I felt like beating him against a tree limb.

A quiet moment at the table was accompanied by the distant whine of an outboard motor on the lake. "Well I hope Art isn't still boring you with business talk out here," Betsy Guilafante said upon returning to the table, "We're here on vacation, Art. Remember?"

The Big A snickered out loud, as if chuckling at the thought of anyone taking a vacation.

"Let me guess…" I glowered at him, "Vacations don't make money either."

My dad choked on another chip before rushing a hand to my shoulder. His face became the picture of confusion. He was wrestling over which was more important at that moment, asking someone to give him the Heimlich or stopping his daughter from embarrassing his entire family in front of their new neighbors.

"I like that one, Walt," Art said, nodding his big eyes in my direction. "She's a real firecracker!"

I looked away quickly, not wanting the Big A to like me. I'd rather stare down a seventy-mile an hour Roni Bonafetti dodge ball filled with concrete than have the Big A like me. And don't think for a moment Roni couldn't hurl a concrete dodgeball, because she absolutely could.

The busy little wings of the swallows caught my eye again. They were still pumping away. Diving low to drink from the lake, their forked tails silhouetted against the sky. One swooped beneath the wing of Art Guilafante's giant, too-big-for-Bass-Lake plane.

I stared at the plane. The grotesquely enormous machine that had nearly ground my brother and I up like raw hamburger. Rolling gently on the waves, it bobbed silently in the shadows of the gathering darkness looking harmless now, but I knew better. The floatplane was like its pilot; loud, obnoxious and unwelcome.

That night I sat with my arms on the sill of my window looking down at the lake. The dark shadow of a lone pontoon crawled across the water. A soft breeze stirred my hair. In the growing darkness, campfires dotted the shoreline. I could see families circling their fire pits, roasting marshmallows and sharing stories from another day on the water. Their faint sound of laughter drifted over the water.

Against the fading light, the trees of the swamp rose like jagged mountain peaks. I thought about the heron mothers, warming their young against the chill of the night. In my head I could hear the haunting call of the little screech owl Grandpa Tug and I both loved. This was the place the backside of the Big A's precious golf course would one day stand?

A full moon hung low in the sky, but my thoughts were wrapped around Art Guilafante. His cheesy smile. His Too-Big-for-Bass-Lake floatplane. His plans for draining the swamp and the uncomfortable way he liked to wink. Grandpa always said people only wink when they're hiding something.

I thought about what Weird Harold said the night we arrived. How 'nothing ever stays the same'. Who knew a man that collected Keep Out signs and enjoyed exercising his taxidermy could be so prophetic? In my mind I saw the Big A's bulldozers belching black smoke, crushing trees into dust beneath their tracks.

Suddenly I could hear Grandpa telling a joke. The one about the elephant and the sun block. I could see him raking logs around the fire pit with his trusty seven iron. That's what the lake was. It wasn't about championship golf courses and luxury housing.

In all my happy memories of Bass Lake, there had been no Art Guilafantes. There had been no floatplanes, and there had definitely been no plans for developing the far side of the lake. Someone had to stop all this.

And by someone I certainly didn't mean Kyle. He was busy sawing logs in his bed. I was sure he was lost in his dreams, riding shotgun with Indiana Jones in the cockpit of the Big A's floatplane.

"Grandpa Tug." I started softly, closing my eyes, "I'm not sure if you know this or not, but there's real trouble on the lake. You've gotta do something. Just make the Big A go away before he changes everything. Make him turn that thundering dinosaur with wings around and fly away from here. Just find a way to stop him. Oh yeah, and you've got to get the Trash Queen out of the swamp, or I'm never going to find a glossy ibis. Make her stay away, or at least make it so she can't sing anymore." I shuddered while finishing, "Her voice sounds like a fistful of nails being dragged across a pane of glass. Thanks G'Pa."

I closed my eyes and listened. Outside the wind stirred the leaves in the coffee trees. I waited for the sound, the sound of a voice I just knew would come. And when it did, it would be Grandpa Tug saying, "Sure thing, Jitterbug, whatever you want."

5

~~~~~~~

I laid there motionless...on the ground...there wasn't a stitch of breath in my lungs. The sun, big, round, and full of promise, hung over me. Promising a new day, one filled with laughter and grilled hot dogs and fun in the water. A day where no planes would come after me, screaming down from the sky like a peregrine falcon. One without ominous warnings from creepy neighbors.

But now, I was just numb. I saw the faces of my dad and sister, but they were blurred. I saw them speaking, their lips moving frantically, but I heard nothing. Kyle was there too, hovering over me while zooming in and out with his camera. Was this what it was like to die? There were so many things I hadn't done yet. I wanted to finish middle school, graduate from college, turn thirteen and hit Roni Bonafetti between the eyes with a dodgeball, just once.

"Kayla!" my dad shrieked. "Are you all right!?"

His voice hit me like a pair of shock paddles, causing my heart to start back up. All my senses rushed back as the world became filled with sound again. My dad was frantic, running his hands up and down my legs as if looking for shattered bones.

I had swung from that rope swing at least a hundred times, never dreaming this was possible. Kyle and Abby worked to roll the tire from my chest when I first heard the voice. Thundering and orderly, like an authority figure demanding some explanation, it was the big, dumb voice of Art Guilafante. "What's going on here!?" it seemed to growl as if I'd been swinging on his tire. Then, like a shadow eclipsing the sun, Art Guilafante's enormous face slid into view. Kyle slowly lowered his camera and stood in awe while taking in the giant figure that was our new neighbor.

Many years before that moment, Grandpa Tug had hung a rope from the branch of a silver maple along shore. He fashioned the swing using the tire from an old pick-up truck, and while nobody could vouch for the safety of his contraption, that thing had brought my family years of non-stop, and non-dangerous, entertainment.

There had been hundreds, if not thousands of trips out over the water on his swing. Grandpa Tug kept an old Jack Nicklaus edition seven iron, the same one he stirred the fire with, propped against the trunk. It was the perfect length for reaching out over the water to reel the swing in.

Just minutes before, my brother, ever the athletic showman, had done something resembling a somersault from the swing. My dad was so heavy he'd sent a mushroom cloud of water soaring into the air. We'd even goaded Abby into riding it, though it had felt like convincing a turtle to hurry up.

First the Queen had to put her hair up, wrap her shoes and sunglasses in her towel, then she needed to check the water temperature with her toes. Her routine was exhausting.

When it was my turn, I made three trips out over the water building up speed. I imagined Grandpa Tug doing one of his famous double atomic bombs, but during my final return over land, the old limb groaned as if protesting all this physical activity.

The groan was followed by a sudden clap of thunder. The limb snapped. The rope went limp in my hands before momentum carried my feet over my head. As if being dropped to the rock hard ground on my back wasn't bad enough, this was followed by the heavy truck tire crushing my chest.

Now there I lay, with Art Guilafante standing over me. "What happened?" he asked.

"I'm not sure- but I think I'm dead," I groaned, my arms and legs sprawled out on the grass, motionless, like the chalk outline of a dead body from one of those detective shows on TV.

I felt the Big A's hands probing my arm for a break. His big eyes set about working me over as if he were a medically trained professional instead of just a really big, annoying neighbor bent on destroying all that was sacred to me.

He took a break from diagnosing me long enough to state the obvious, "Looks like the tree limb broke." Art's eyes pointed at the shards of wood sticking out from where the limb had ripped apart moments before.

Ever the master of the obvious, my dad felt the need to add his own opinion, "It's been there thirty years or more. It was bound to break sometime."

They announced their decisions as if they'd cracked some great unsolvable mystery like the translation of Hieroglyphics or discovering the gene that makes all boys think farting is hilarious.

"If it were me, Walt, I'd tear that tree out," the Big A advised, his big hands working the trunk. "Most of the limbs are dead anyway. It's really more of a liability than anything."

Unbelievable! There he went again. Tearing something down every chance he got. When would enough be enough? The man was like a general whose army was already destroying the far side of the lake. Did he really feel the need to wage war against our side too?

"Why tear down a perfectly good tree!?" I asked. "It may be dead, but stuff can still live inside it!" I felt like yelling the words, but my lungs were still flat, so they leaked out as an angry whisper.

"Trees get old, sweetheart," Art explained in a calm tone. He finished his thought with a sudden and somewhat strange grin, "and when they do, they tend to fall over and hurt people."

My face burned. Art Guilafante calling me sweetheart was the only thing on the lake creepier than Weird Harold.

"When they die, they're worthless, and we cut them down."

Art Guilafante's advice sparked memories of Grandma Minnie. How she loved sitting under that tree. I'd seen pictures of her watching the water-skiers from her swing. A swing that was always parked in the shade of the very silver maple Big Art Guilafante was now lobbying to turn in to two by fours, toothpicks, coffee tables, and baseball bats. Was there no end to the manner in which this man could annoy me?

"Your airplane sure is cool, Mr. Guilafante," my brother said unexpectedly. "Reminds me of the Waco Bi-plane from *Raiders of the Lost Ark*."

Here I was, his closest sister, moments away from death, and my brother couldn't quit drooling over that stupid airplane. I wanted to kick him, but the feeling still hadn't returned to my legs yet.

"That's the DHC Otter," Art answered, turning his attention to his floating pride and joy next door.

"DHC?" Dad repeated with a twinge of confusion.

"Stands for de Havilland Canada. They're pretty much the standard bearers of short-take-off-and-landing aircraft. The Beaver really put them on the map. Of course, both are a lot more functional than the Waco. The Otter alone has a range of almost 1,000 miles on a single tank of fuel."

I was seething. Otters? Beavers? Art Guilafante wouldn't know a beaver if one came up and gnawed half his leg off. "Well I guess if you ever decide to sell your cottage and move away, it's good to know you could haul a lot of stuff a long, long, *long* way away from here," I suggested in a manner intended to be as obvious as possible.

"Either way, that's sure some seaplane you've got there Art," my dad said, changing the conversation while throwing darts at me with his eyes. I'll admit, Dad did have some impressive conflict resolution skills.

"Technically it's a floatplane, Walt," Art corrected, "I'm afraid a seaplane would be far too big for a tiny lake like this!"

I raised my head to let Art know most people on the lake believed his floatplane was too big as well, but felt Dad's hand land on my shoulder.

"Maybe I'll take you up sometime, Kyle," Art offered. "If it's all right with your dad of course!"

"Wow, Dad! Can I? Can I really? I mean is it okay if I go flying with Mr. Big A?"

"Hello?" I interrupted suddenly. "What about me? You know, the one that almost died? Does anyone care that I may never move again?"

"Sorry, Kay. Does anything hurt?" my dad asked, turning his attention back to me.

"Just my entire body. That's all," I answered.

"Really?" Abby snarked, ramming her hands into her hips, "because from here it looks like the only thing that's bruised is your ego."

"She'll be fine, Walt. There doesn't appear to be any internal bleeding, and nothing's broken."

"Thanks for coming over, Art," my dad said, placing a hand on the man's big shoulder.

"That's what neighbors are for," Art answered offering another disturbing wink.

I almost gagged. What was with this guy and winking? It was a *really* annoying habit. As Art stood up to leave us, I watched him crossing Lake Road with his long, Sasquatch-like gait.

From his white plastic lawn chair, I could tell Weird Harold Farcus had been watching it all, too; a crooked eye bent beneath that floppy bucket hat. The look on his face was clear, after forty years on the lake he'd seen that tree survive everything: freezing winters, scorching summers, powerful windstorms. Never in a million years did he think a branch could just fall off like that. There was no mistaking it. Even Weird Harold found this turn of events quite weird indeed, perhaps suspicious even. Big Art Guilafante had been at the lake only two days, and in that time I had almost died twice.

Part of me, the one I got from my dad most likely, accepted the accidents as odd twists of fate. The other part of me, the one I got from my mom, even though she always said it came from Dad, told me there was trouble.

That afternoon I wanted to get as far away from our new neighbors as I could, so I pedaled my way back to the swamp. It was a harder ride this time because my chest was still sore, and I couldn't draw a deep breath. Being the middle of the day, I knew the odds of finding an ibis there would be unlikely, but the swamp was still the best place to go when you needed to collect your thoughts.

I remembered the time Jimmy Longstockings wanted to cut down a bunch of trees around his cottage. Grandpa Tug had got real mad and asked Jimmy not to. Jimmy didn't trust the old trees and was afraid one would come crashing through the roof of his cottage. "Go mind your own business, Tug!" Jimmy had yelled across his yard. That's when Grandpa took me to the swamp, so he could cool down. We spent the day counting warblers and in the end Jimmy didn't cut any of his trees down, which made Grandpa and me very happy.

Now I stood ankle deep in the mucky water, listening to the swamp breathe. The chittering of the wrens and knocking of the woodpeckers swirled around me. The canopy of the swamp had turned the world to dusk as a sensation of coolness crept over me.

Buried in the bark of a towering swamp cottonwood, I found the square holes where a pileated had been digging for ants. And while there were plenty of signs of the ibis along shore, I felt better knowing there were no signs of the Trash Queen. This is what the swamp was supposed to be, my own secret world.

I let Grandpa's swamp log fall open to a random page. The entry was about a yellow rail, a very rare bird he had only seen once in the swamp. The entry read: 'Saw a male scurrying for cover north of Mentone's oak. Heard him many times before, he loves it here. So many places to hide!"

Eric Walker Williams

The championship golf course Art wanted so badly would one day cover the exact spot in which I stood. I could see empty beer cans and discarded cigarette butts littered amongst the clusters of cinnamon ferns. A river of pesticides and herbicides would soon flow where once herons had strutted in the shallows.

I wanted Grandpa Tug to stop all this. Why wasn't he doing more? There was no way he would ever let Art bulldoze this place. Grandpa Tug was the strongest man I knew. He was stronger than Big Art's float plane and stronger than his bulldozers and earth movers. Grandpa was stronger than that maple branch and Roni Bonafetti's arm put together. I knew he loved this place more than life itself. There was no way he could just sit back and let Art destroy it all. If Grandpa was going to come back and do something, now was the time, because if he waited much longer, it would be too late.

But still, what was he waiting for? Art was getting closer every day to destroying the swamp. Where was Grandpa Tug? Suddenly I felt helpless. Art's bulldozers and earthmovers were on the horizon, rolling in like a July thunderstorm. I could feel the power of it all and never before had I felt so small.

6

~~~~~~~

The old wooden garage door creaked and groaned as dad hoisted it up. Shafts of sunlight streamed into the dark and dusty shed, making it look more like an Egyptian tomb. The scent of gasoline and teak oil filled my nostrils.

"There she is," Dad said, beaming. "Grandpa's Toy. Hasn't changed a bit right? Just look at her, Kay. Got a little dust on her now, but somehow she still shines."

Sunlight sparkled off the chrome navigation light. Deep in the dark wood of the hull, my reflection came back as faded and faint. The trailer was rusted and the tires were bald. The wheel cover squeaked when I climbed up to look inside.

My eyes fell on the familiar pearl-white steering wheel nestled amongst the chrome instrument panel and red-leather bench seat Grandpa Tug had manned for so many years. Now that seat had never looked so empty. A part of me still thought we'd find Grandpa tinkering in the shed when Dad raised the door. He was an expert at moving junk from one corner to the other to make room for more, but now everything was just quiet. The lake was a black and white world

Eric Walker Williams

now. The bench on the pier was cold and the seat in Grandpa's Toy was empty.

"This was Grandpa Tug's baby. I can't tell you how many sunsets she drug me into," Dad explained. "Safe to say they don't make them like this anymore."

She'd been christened Grandpa's Toy. Now it was the only wooden boat left on Bass Lake, a seventeen foot, 1954 Chris Craft Sportsman that Grandpa Tug loved like a child.

"Did I ever tell you I used to ski on Grandpa's back?" Dad asked, his eyes drifting away.

"Only like a million times," the Queen huffed in an unimpressed manner.

Teenagers seemed eternally unimpressed. Abby could see a lion do a back flip while juggling flaming sticks of dynamite and would probably just yawn and ask where the concession stand was.

"He used to make me wear this old red helmet. I'm sure it's around here somewhere. Boy he loved to ski," Dad said. "It's been a few years, so the boys over at the marina are going to check her out first thing in the morning. When they're done with her, we can get out on the water. It's about time you guys learned."

"And by 'you guys' you mean Kyle and Abby right?" I asked quickly.

"I mean all three of you. It's time, Kay. You can't keep coming down here if you're not going to ski. It's against the rules."

Hearing Dad's words sent me back to the water with Grandpa Tug. The same hopeless feeling rushed over me. Struggling to keep the skis together, fighting to stay upright in the water. It was all so hard. I just couldn't do it. Learning to waterski was on the same level with climbing Mount Everest or swimming across Lake Michigan.

Beyond the fact learning seemed nearly impossible, I also didn't know how I felt about trying again. Grandpa's Toy had never looked so old and worn out. It was an artifact from Grandpa Tug's world, and though I was clearly standing with my hand on it, that place seemed a million miles away now.

In the morning, I found Mom in the kitchen busy boxing up some of Grandpa's old stuff. The table was clogged with boxes. Words like 'old pants' and 'summer wear' had been written on them. "Gonna be a hot one today," she said, stopping to pour a glass of orange juice for me, "I've got to tackle that garden sometime, might as well be today. It looks like there's stuff growing back there, I just need to clear out the weeds. Can you believe that? Nobody's been up here for two years and there's still stuff growing out there? Hey, you never told me if you found anything in the swamp?"

"Just some strange old lady."

"Really? What was she doing there?"

"Picking up trash."

"In the swamp? Really? Well, that's a very nice thing to do."

"It's not nice, Mom. She's loud. And she sings songs! And they're way off key! Her voice is like a cross between a screeching cat, a freight train, and someone playing a guitar with a violin bow."

"Wow, that was pretty specific."

"I'm never going to find an ibis with that woman around!"

Eric Walker Williams

"Well, at least it sounds like someone's been watching the swamp with you and Grandpa gone for the last couple years."

"Boat's hooked up to the Jeep. Let's take her over to the marina and let the boys give her a tune up," Dad said, dumping what was left of his coffee into the sink before setting his empty mug on the window sill.

"Can we stop at the grocery? I need a couple things."

"Sounds good. Abby!" he yelled up the stairs. "Your mom and I are leaving, we'll be back in an hour or so. Keep an eye on your brother and sister while we're gone okay?"

Keep an eye on us? As in Kyle and me? He expected Abby to keep an eye on us? I almost gagged. Her idea of watching us was to put her earbuds in and stick her nose in a magazine. Anybody who spent five minutes in the same room with Abby would soon realize she shouldn't be trusted to watch a bowl of fruit left on the kitchen table. Not to mention she had these incredibly ridiculous teenager rules, like making Kyle and me arm-wrestle for the right to get a soda out of the fridge for her or granting us the 'privilege' of cleaning up her nasty toe-garbage. Just in case you haven't experienced nasty toe-garbage, it's the disgusting fungus that builds up between my sister's toes. It's a strange concoction of lint, sweat, dirt, and various bacteria yet to be identified by the scientific world.

When she heard the cottage door close, the Queen of Hormonestan immediately shouted down the stairs, "Hey, turd-brains! You two can't look at me while Mom and Dad are gone unless you ask for permission first!"

It was too early in the morning to be dealing with my sister, so I darted for the hammock in the front yard. Across the lake the silver maples were fluttering again. A strong wind from the west was turning their leaves from green to a silver brighter than Christmas tinsel.

Then, from behind the Indian grass along shore, the same two swallows I'd seen the day before appeared. As they chased each other around in frantic circles, I decided they needed names. The little male seemed to be brave and proud, which meant he sounded like a Bud. The female was more delicate and beautiful. She looked like an Ella. Bud skimmed the water, snapping a bug from the surface. The two met in midair before turning back toward Art Guilafante's cottage.

Grandpa always said the same swallows returned to the lake every spring. Some wintered as far away as Venezuela, but they always came back. In the swallows' world it was the job of the male to find a good nesting spot before the female agreed to join him. Apparently Art Guilafante's cottage was the good nesting spot Bud had found, because soon they both disappeared into a nest under Art's eave.

"Hey Kay!" My brother's voice screeched from behind the cottage, "Come in here!"

I raced to the shed. With the boat gone, the guts of the little garage were now visible. For years it had laid like a lion in the weeds, waiting to swallow up any old furniture that dared to stray from the cottage. The walls were covered with water skis, jackets, helmets, inner tubes, and old fishing equipment. The floor was littered with dusty lamps, mismatched lawn chairs, a handful of old paint cans, and the occasional five gallon bucket.

"It's like some kind of nautical museum in here," Kyle said, using his foot to push a cardboard box out of his way. That's when I saw it. Dad's old red helmet. I picked it up and blew some dust off it.

Eric Walker Williams

This was my chance. My chance to finally make Grandpa happy by skiing. Well, you know, skiing without actually having to get in the water, be pulled by a boat or hit by another boat or, you know, risking the chance I might drown.

We made busy rummaging around the shed. "Kay, I know this is going to sound super-crazy, but if there's any way we can try to recreate you falling from the rope swing later, I'd love to get some footage for *The Curse of Bass Lake*."

"You're joking, right?" I asked, strapping Dad's helmet on. "I mean you don't actually think I'm going to recreate an accident that could have just as easily killed me."

"What's with the helmet? You climbing Everest or something?"

I shot Kyle a look as we continued inspecting the contents of the shed. "You know, none of the accidents you see in the movies are real," he explained, "There's a lot we can do to make it seem like you fell from the rope swing without you actually falling from the rope swing again. It's all about close ups and camera angles. I'm picturing this great arc shot with you lying in the grass."

Before I could tell Kyle how long the odds were that I was going to ever go near that rope swing again, I spotted two life belts nestled under the workbench.

"Come on, let's waterski!" I said, fishing the belts out to strap one on.

"You don't need a helmet to water ski."

"You do if you're going to ski on someone's back! We need life vests too." I said, handing one of the belts to Kyle.

He held the little white belt up. "These are life vests?"

"They're called life-belts. Dad used them when he was our age. I think they're illegal now or something."

Kyle shoved his feet into a pair of skis I'd laid out on the floor, and stepped toward a stepladder, swinging his feet around more awkwardly than a scuba diver in flippers. Soon enough I had scaled the stepladder and was perched on his shoulders. "Hit it!" I commanded as if Kyle were both driving the boat and riding water skis simultaneously.

With knees bent low, he started bobbing left and right, gurgling out loud. Apparently, when I suggested he make a sound like Grandpa's Toy, he heard 'make a sound like a garbage disposal trying to eat an aluminum can'.

"Lean to the left a bit," he ordered in such a fashion one might actually believe he'd skied with someone on his shoulders before. "Now to the right."

I leaned over imagining Grandpa Tug waving at me from the driver's seat. He was so proud of me for being brave enough to ski on someone's back. Before I could wave back however, I started to lose balance.

The first thing my hands caught was an old rope attached to the overhead door. When I grabbed it, the door groaned loudly. I pulled harder on the rope, trying to right myself on Kyle's shoulders. A loud snap was heard before the shed began to shake as if an earthquake was hitting the lake. Bolts began popping off the door. The left side broke free first, causing the door to sag awkwardly. Then in a massive clap of thunder, the door fell from the ceiling, burying us like an avalanche.

After the explosion of the falling door had echoed across the lake, silence returned to the old shed. Only the rattling sound of a few stray bolts on the concrete was heard.

"What the heck?" Abby wailed upon arriving. Through the shards of what had been our overhead door, I saw Abby's hands trying to part the cloud of dust hiding the remainder of the shed. "Kyle? Kayla? You in here?"

Kyle's voice groaned from beneath the door, "You all right, sis?"

"I have a garage door on top of me," I gasped softly, "so I've been better."

"I can't believe this! I leave you two alone for thirty seconds, and *this* is what happens!?" Abby barked. "Mom and dad are going to *kill* me!!"

"You? What about us? We're lucky we weren't killed!" I snapped back.

Kyle and I were both lying on the floor of the shed, heads sticking out from under that garage door as if someone had tucked us into bed by covering us up with it. Despite the fact we could have easily been crushed, everything was pretty much fine until he showed up. That's when it happened. Of all the people I *didn't* want to see at that moment, there he was. Those big eyes glaring down at me again. From the doorway of the shed, Art Guilafante cast his big shadow over us.

7

~~~~~~

"What happened here!?" Art thundered, latching his big hands on the edge of the door. In the blink of an eye he had whipped the door off us and thrown it down in the yard, as if he were tossing an empty pizza box into the trash.

"I could hear the crash all the way down by the water! Are you two all right?" The Big A knelt beside us, so close I could smell the onions he'd had for lunch. Smothering my face, even Art's breath was heavy.

Kyle rolled over, feet still in the skis. When I sat up, Dad's plastic red helmet sat sideways on my head.

"Yeah, we're okay." I announced quickly, in the hopes Art would lose interest and leave.

"What were you two doing anyway?" Abby asked.

"Skiing," Kyle answered, his face pasted with a dusty layer of grime.

"Really? Uh…most people prefer to do that on the water," Abby pointed out. "Good thing you had your powdered donuts on though!"

"Actually, it would have been better had they both been wearing helmets," the Big A explained, totally missing my sister's attempt at humor. "The way that door fell, Kyle's lucky he wasn't seriously hurt. He could have a concussion or fractured skull. In fact, if it had hit him just right, the door might have punctured a lung or broken his spine. There's just no end to what could have happened."

Art reached one of his giant paws down to help me up. He kept his large round eyes trained on my every move. In my head I heard his voice saying 'When trees get old, they fall over and hurt people.'

I didn't want the Big A's help. If I let him help me off the floor, what was next? Taking a ride in his Too-Big-for-Bass-Lake-Float-Plane? Bulldozing a row of silver maples or maybe helping him dynamite some mallard nests? No, I wouldn't have any of it. I rolled over quickly and pulled myself back to my feet.

My P.E. teacher likes to say I'm "made of nothin' and full of determination". She saw me take that Roni Bonafetti dodge ball between the eyes. She saw it lay me out on the gym floor, and she'd blushed when I fought back to my feet and told her I was staying in the game.

"What happened?" My mom's voice rang out upon arriving. "Is everyone all right!?"

"They're fine," Abby answered. "The garage door just fell on them. That's all."

"That's all!?" Mom choked.

"The supports for the door gave out, Kathy. Looks like most of these rafters are rotten. If it were me, I'd tear this old shed down."

There Art went again. Offering to tear something down or rip something out. Always wanting to change things. Why couldn't he just leave everything alone?

"I can't believe this happened!" Mom shrieked, "I'm gone a half an hour, and the garage door falls on you? Abby, your father told you to keep an eye on them!"

"What did you want me to do, Mom? Catch the door before it fell on their heads? I'm not Superwoman!"

"We'll talk about this later, young lady!" Mom snapped, her face turning red.

Abby rolled her eyes as Art went on. "You know, sometimes these old properties can be dangerous. Weathered boards, rusty nails, rotted foundations. If a person's not careful, they can get hurt *real* bad."

As if it ran on electricity and someone had just ripped the cord from a wall socket, my heart stopped dead in my chest. Did he *really* just say that? Did the Big A really just say there was a chance I could get hurt real bad?

A quiet moment lingered. From the lake came the distant whine of a pontoon motor. Nobody spoke, but I knew everyone was thinking the exact same thing.

Still, standing there with a collapsed shed door nearby, I couldn't help but wonder why Grandpa Tug was letting all this happen to me. Three potentially dangerous accidents in two days. Grandpa had always looked out for me. He had always protected me, and now, when I needed him most, he was nowhere to be found.

"Thanks for being here, Art," Mom finally said. "I hope it wasn't too much trouble for you."

"Nothing any good neighbor wouldn't have done," the Big A answered, placing his hand on my mom's shoulder as if they were long lost relatives.

"Thanks, Art. Kids, you wait here. I'm going inside to get the first aid kit."

Without speaking, Art turned away and left us. In long, careful strides, the man walked back to his cottage.

"Kay," Kyle began softly, "Remember what you said in the swamp? How there wasn't any danger or suspense on the lake?"

Still stunned, I nodded my head slowly.

"Looks like you were wrong."

I almost tossed my cookies. Kyle was right. The lake was turning out to be a dangerous place. I looked for the white bucket hat of Weird Harold Farcus and found him standing in the middle of Lake Road. From under the brim of that hat he was peering up the drive into our shed. Our eyes met, and I found a cagey gleam staring back at me. Could we be thinking the same thing? Was it possible Weird Harold thought the Big A was bad news as well?

I mean here I'd survived three near death accidents in two days, and Art was one of the first to show up each time? It was all starting to come into focus. The edges were still blurred and uneven, but I was sharp enough to know what I was looking at. This was more than just an obnoxious neighbor rushing to help out. This was more than just a coincidence. Either the Big A was like Superman and had a knack for being around whenever bad things happened, or he was trying to kill us.

8

~~~~~~~

"Ghost man on first and second," Kyle announced, bouncing his big red bat on the Frisbee marking home plate.

From the pitcher's mound, I stood with the Wiffle Ball in my hands. The sun felt hot on my neck. Kyle's face was bent in concentration while waving the bat over his head.

I thought Wiffle Ball would help take my mind off all that had happened, but no matter how hard I tried, I couldn't shake the collapsing shed door. My chest felt heavy, as if it were still lying on top of me. The thunderous sound of the supports shattering echoed in my head and I could still feel the creepiness of Big Art Guilafante standing over me.

"This may sound crazy, but don't you think it's a little bit strange that all these accidents have happened since we came back?"

"I just can't believe three have happened and I don't have footage of any of them. A docudrama is only as good as its authentic footage. I mean there's freedom as a film-maker to recreate things through dialogue and acting, but in the end reality serves as the center of any award-winning docudrama. It's always the real history that draws people in."

"But what about Art? Isn't it weird he's been around *every* time something has happened? I mean, what are the odds he would just happen to be watching or be nearby?"

Everything flashed through my mind at once. The floatplane, the rope swing, and the collapsing shed door. They were all potentially fatal accidents and Art had been witness to each of them. "I just think it has to be more than just a coincidence," I confessed, "I mean am I crazy to think he's trying to hurt us?"

"No. It's not crazy. Crazy was the Joker in *Batman* or Lotso in *Toy Story*. I mean, trust me when I say you're nothing like those two."

"Thanks, I think. But, I just can't help thinking that, for some reason, Art doesn't want us on the lake. What about you? I mean, you were there for all of them too. Is it just a crazy idea to think Art doesn't want us around?"

"No." Kyle answered quickly, bouncing his bat off the Frisbee again, "It was a crazy idea for Lex Luthor to think he could use a nuclear bomb to get rid of California, maybe even crazier for him to think Superman wouldn't wind up stopping him."

Before Kyle could finish his thought, the front door of Art's cottage slammed shut. The Big A came lumbering out. Grabbing a ladder from his deck, he turned toward a tree in his front yard.

"Ghost man on first and second!" I yelled, trying to hide the fact we'd been talking about our neighbor.

Watching Art plodding through the grass with those big bare feet of his made the hair on the back of my neck stand on end. For a moment, I threw darts at him with my eyes. I was on to Art Guilafante. He may have been tall and successful and owned his own company and airplane, but he had no idea who he was messing with.

This lake belonged to my family. Grandpa Tug had put roots down here long before Art Guilafante had ever even found it on a map. It was going to take more than a falling rope swing and brush with a shed door for my family to turn tail and run. Summoning all the strength I had, my face swelled with determination as I went into my wind up.

For one fleeting moment, I was Roni Bonafetti, the Dodge Ball Queen, blessed with the arm of a Greek god. That's when I threw the ball as hard as I could. Kyle immediately jumped on my pitch and sent a towering shot over my head. I watched the ball screaming through the air as if propelled by a rocket. I'd never seen him hit one so far. "That's three runs!!" He screamed, "Seven-*nothing*!!"

As he rounded the bases, Kyle was making fake crowd noise and pumping a fist in the air. He looked like he was having an arm cramp or reaction to some bad food.

"All right, all right already, we know the score!" I shouted, making no effort to hide how completely annoyed I was.

"Hurry up and get the ball. I'm gonna crank another one!" he shouted, snatching his bat up before banging it on the Frisbee again to make ready for the next pitch.

"I can't," I answered weakly. Kyle's boisterous celebrating faded when he saw me standing at the edge of Weird Harold's yard. The ball had gone *over* the redwood fence outlining his property.

Slowly Kyle drifted to my side. We stood together as if the edge of our yard was the edge of the world. Neither of us dared to venture another step.

The grass in Harold's yard was knee high. An old bicycle with rusted fenders had been laid to rest against the fence. Ivy was winding through the spokes as if trying to reach the seat for one final attempt at escaping Harold's yard.

Another large and crooked KEEP OUT sign hung next to the gap in his fence where a gate once stood. Empty five gallon buckets and Styrofoam bait coolers were strewn everywhere. They appeared in a totally random pattern, as if arranged by a tornado.

In the front window of Harold's cottage I found the craggy branch, and this time the opossum was back. Large and round, he was posed with a front claw up in the air, his tiny eyes narrowed at me in rage. Apparently he didn't like Wiffle balls, because his jaws were wide open and his fangs were bared as if he were a man-eater.

In the middle of this mess, Harold and his white bucket hat remained planted in his three legged plastic lawn chair, a mere two feet from our ball. Kyle's home run had fallen right in front of him, yet there he sat motionless, as if carved from stone.

I realized Minnix Family Wiffle Ball Rules clearly stated that whoever was playing the field was responsible for retrieving all balls put into play, but none of that mattered now. After hearing so many strange stories about the Farcus family, I'd decided I'd rather belly crawl across a field of Chinese armor tailed scorpions than walk into Harold's yard.

Kyle and I turned our backs to Harold's cottage to plot our next move.

"Where's the ball?" He whispered.

"You cleared the fence. It's right in front of him."

"Okay, so what do we do now?"

"How should I know? You hit a home run I can't get to, that means you have to go after it."

Kyle's face bent with concentration as he considered his options. "Okay, tell me everything you know about an opossum."

"What? Why?"

"The opossum, you know? The one in the window? If I know some stuff about it, maybe I can distract him with conversation long enough to get the ball back."

I paused to collect my thoughts. It wasn't that great of an idea, but it was all we had. "Well, I know they're really susceptible to frostbite because their ears are naked."

"Naked?"

"Yeah, you know? They don't have any fur? They can also squeeze through a hole smaller than a softball and they like to hole up in bad weather."

"Okay, that's a start," Kyle said as we broke our huddle and turned back toward Harold's fence. When we did, Harold Farcus was standing on the other side, so close I could smell the spearmint on his breath. He was staring at us, a lifeless look in his eyes, and our Wiffle ball in his hands.

Eric Walker Williams

9

~~~~~~~

"That was a nice home run kid," Weird Harold wheezed in a raspy voice. "You've got a good swing."

As he handed the ball to Kyle, my eyes couldn't leave the man. This was the first time I'd seen him up close in the daylight. Harold Farcus was a dog-faced man. Wiry and rail thin, his clothes sagged on his frame.

His teeth, stained the color of apple cider, were long and pointy, not unlike those of a woodchuck, and appeared sharp enough to gnaw through a telephone pole. The man's cheeks were littered with dark stubble and his slanted silver eyes were filled with a faraway look.

Did he always look so serious? I tried to imagine Weird Harold smiling. What it might be like to see him laughing. For Harold, smiling of any sort was apparently reserved for special occasions only, like if he saw a dog being run over or a small child being carried off by a great horned owl.

I looked at my brother. I could read his face clearly. In his head he was repeating the words, "Don't call him weird, don't call him weird."

"Thanks Weir-thanks Har-thanks Mr. Farcus." Kyle finished, about as smoothly as a cheese grater.

In my head I could hear my mom shrieking over the thought of us talking to Harold. For years she'd warned us about talking to him. She had this rehearsed speech she always gave about Harold not practicing hygiene or turning lights on in his cottage after dark or licking beans from a soup can.

Despite her warning, I still couldn't move. I wanted to turn and run, but just like that day in the water with the Big A's Too-Big-for-Bass-Lake Floatplane bearing down on me, my body wouldn't budge.

"Sure've been some awful strange things goin' on lately," Harold offered.

Nobody answered. Kyle and I stood shoulder to shoulder at the fence, staring back at Weird Harold as if he were speaking Mandarin Chinese.

"Never seen the luck you've had though…"

My pulse quickened as Weird Harold went on, "That old maple tree was one of the strongest on the lake. She could've survived a hurricane. And that shed, well nobody could build one stronger than Tug Minnix. No sir, there've been some downright strange things goin' on 'round here."

Somehow I was starting to find Harold Farcus less and less weird, even though he had yet to look me in the eye. How was this possible? Here was a man who rarely spoke and never changed clothes, a man everyone on the lake regarded as a wild-eyed recluse who cut his grass only once a year and smelled of rotting fish, and yet somehow, he suddenly seemed to be the most normal person around.

"Larry thinks it all has something to do with that city feller showing up next door…the one with the plane. Larry don't like planes…"

"Larry?" I repeated. Harold had mentioned a Larry the night we first arrived. I remembered him saying, 'Red sky at night, Larry, no need to hole up tonight'. It had seemed so weird at the time because there was nobody else around.

Harold nodded toward his window. My eyes fell on the opossum again. His bright pink nose was suddenly aimed in my direction. His dark beady eyes glowered at me. I didn't know what to do. I'd never been in a staring contest with a stuffed opossum before.

"Is your opossum named Larry?" I asked.

Harold didn't answer. He just stood staring across his weedy lawn toward the lake.

It all made sense now. Grandpa Tug was always saying opossums liked to hunker down when bad weather rolled in. The call of the rain crow alone was usually enough to send one scurrying for cover. That's why Harold had said what he did. He was trying to comfort Larry.

"Were you taking him for a walk yesterday? Down by the lake?" I asked.

"Larry likes to get out once in a while. Says sometimes he feels cooped up and needs some fresh air," Harold answered, still refusing to make eye contact with us.

Kyle's eyes were locked on the animal. He began making quick motions with his hands, trying to get the opossum to react. "Does Larry ever move? Or is he just like, scared or something? " Kyle asked, throwing a couple strange faces back at the creature.

"Don't let 'em fool you," Harold responded suddenly. "He may not get around like he used to, but Larry don't miss much up here. He sees everything. And he ain't too sure about that new feller next door. The one from the city."

My eyes drifted back to Larry. He was still perched on the tree limb in Harold's front window, overlooking the lake with his nose pointed to the sky.

"Says he's got a real bad feeling about him."

"You mean, Art?" I asked quickly.

Harold pointed the slits of his eyes toward the Big A's cottage where Art was busy working in his yard. "Just look at him. Feller's so big. If he fell down he'd be halfway home. Larry don't trust him, what with his big, flashy airplane and all them plastic palaces he's buildin' 'cross the lake."

"Why did Jimmy Longstockings sell his cottage to that weirdo anyway?" I blurted before my hand could get to my mouth.

Harold's head swiveled around quickly. A faint chuckle escaped his lungs. "Sold it? That what you think? That Jimmy just took a check and walked away?" Weird Harold's silver eyes flashed at mine quickly, careful not to linger. "No, that ain't how it happened at all. See, ol' Art came at the end of last season wanting to buy Jimmy's place, but Jimmy said no. Art wasn't happy…big spender from the city like that. Fist full of cash. They don't like to hear the word no, so a few weeks later Jimmy's dog turned up missing."

Harold paused to glance back toward his cottage, "Calm down, Larry!" He barked. "I hear you already. Don't let your imagination get the best of you, he ain't listenin' to us. Quit bein' so paranoid."

Kyle was still waving his hands up and down like a complete moron, trying to get Larry's eyes to follow them. Meanwhile Larry was resting motionless in the window, because he was dead.

"Then one night, one of them big Coffee trees fell on Jimmy's shed. Crushed part of the shed, but only missed his bedroom by a few feet."

The thought of a seventy-five foot tall tree smashing Jimmy's cottage left me motionless under Weird Harold's spell. "A week later he sold his place to Art. Art had his crew come down and rebuild part of the shed and put some new siding on the cottage. Larry's not a fan of the color they chose, but what can you do?"

"We think he's trying to kill us!" I burst unexpectedly.

There was no answer from Weird Harold. I waited to find a suspicious look sneaking out from under that white bucket hat, but found only a cold, hard stare. At that point I would have taken anything, a nod in agreement, a pair of wide eyes saying 'me too'. The moment lingered. Somewhere a lawnmower whirred.

My eyes wandered back to the Big A. He was hacking at a tree limb with a hand saw. He stopped long enough to give us a big 'I'm innocent' smile and an 'it's not me' wave before going back to his tree. Art Guilafante was sweating so much his shirt was changing colors. Was this because it was 102 in the shade? Or did Art know we were on to him? I couldn't be sure.

"But why wouldn't Art want us up here?" I asked, hoping Harold would somehow have an answer.

"Windy one out there today, Larry. The bass'l be jumpin' for sure," Harold said staring out across the lake.

There he went again. Changing the course of a conversation without warning. But I wasn't going to let it happen this time. Harold seemed like he wanted to tell us something and he was so close.

"Harold, why do you think Art would want to scare us off the lake?" I asked again.

The man's steely eyes returned from his trip around the lake, "Remember what he said the day he first met you? The way he said 'everything has a price tag'?"

I shuddered. Harold was right. Art had gone on and on about condos making more money than cottages. Every thought that lingered in Art Guilafante's head somehow seemed to be attached to money. "So the Big A wants to buy our cottage so he can put up more of his condos?" I whispered.

"Art's a lot like the kingbird. Doesn't really matter who you are, they don't want you around," Harold answered, leaning against his fence in a tired manner. "He's a pretty smart feller and he can read your dad like a book. Wally's the type who'd get rid of somethin' quick… if it were dangerous to his own kids."

That's when our conversation reached a lull. The world of Bass Lake returned. Sputtering motor boats, honking geese, waves lapping at the shore. Harold and I were on the same page and I wasn't sure how I felt about it. After all, he was the strangest man on the lake, and one I'd been warned my whole life to stay away from.

While I was wrestling with this, Kyle was busy trying to process the fact Larry was still ignoring him and Art Guilafante kept sawing away like the madman that he was. The accidents were starting to make complete sense now.

Watching the Big A hacking away at that limb, I could read his eyes. They were full of pure anger. The kind only a cold-blooded killer could have. There was no doubt now, Art Guilafante was after us. And though he was still a wild-eyed recluse, somewhere beneath the shade of that bucket hat I finally caught a glimpse of Harold Farcus for who he truly was. Harold was with us, the Big A against us and we needed Grandpa Tug now more than ever.

Eric Walker Williams

10
~~~~~~~

"What you have just said is by far the most ridiculous thing I've ever heard!" my dad howled, slamming a fist down so hard on the table he made the silverware jump.

"Calm down, Walter," Abby jumped in. "That vein on your forehead is coming back."

"You stay out of this, young lady, and don't call me Walter!" Dad snapped, pointing a loaded butter knife at my sister.

The vein on the side of Dad's head was bulging. I hadn't seen it since the time Abby said she wanted to be a professional clothes shopper. It was the same vein I'd seen when Kyle flushed Dad's golf hat down the toilet. It wasn't that my dad was overly attached to the golf hat. It's just that Kyle flooded the upstairs of our house, and it cost so much to fix everything that our trip to Disney World got cancelled.

"Pass the rolls please, sweetie," Mom said to Kyle as Dad sat stewing at the end of the table, steam rolling from his ears.

Grandpa Tug said there were always going to be people who don't believe the truth. People who think the moon landing was faked or that the pyramids of Giza were placed there by aliens. These are the very same people who claim to have an uncle who worked with Elvis at a gas station in northern Michigan. Dad didn't waste time on that kind of stuff. He was a no-nonsense, hard-working man who fully believed we landed on the moon, the pyramids were built by slaves and Elvis died on the toilet.

His face burned red as he went on. "In fact, if you find anyone who believes Art Guilafante wants to kill you, tell them I have some oceanfront property in Oklahoma I'm interested in selling!"

"Wait a minute, can we stop for a second?" the Queen said, holding a half-eaten roll up. "Did someone just say there's an ocean in Oklahoma? Why haven't I heard about this before?"

"Hang on," Kyle said, pulling his camera out from under the table. "I want to film this. Everybody just go on as you were. Act natural," He advised, panning around the table slowly. "*The Curse of Bass Lake,* scene three…and, action!"

"Kyle," Dad began slowly, "Put that camera away before I throw it off the wall."

Kyle slowly lowered his camera. "You know Dad, this is the United States of America. We have certain freedoms and rights, one of which is the right to free and open media and one of the most popular forms of media is film."

"And this is my cottage and I bought that camera which means if I want to throw that camera off my cottage wall I can."

"Listen to what you're saying, Kayla. You actually think Art Guilafante wants to kill you?" my mom asked.

"Mom, the guy's been here two days and I've almost died three times."

"And when he came to the shed he went out of his way to tell us he'd been down by the water when the door collapsed," Kyle added. "It's like he knew we suspected him, Mom. It's a well-known fact the bad guy in every movie ever made always has a really weak alibi."

"This isn't a movie, Kyle!" my dad fired back. "Grandpa's cottage is old. Things are going to break from time to time. You know, the tree limb, the garage door. We'll all just have to be more careful that's all."

I thought dinner might be the best place to hash out my theory about Art Guilafante, but it wasn't going as well as I had planned. My parents were dismissing everything as a twelve year old with an overactive imagination.

This had to be more than just a string of bad luck. Something strange was going on at Bass Lake, and nothing Dad could say would convince me otherwise. It really didn't matter if Dad believed me or not because I already had one adult who did.

"I guess you need to sell some of your oceanfront property to Weird Harold then, because he agrees with me," I announced.

"Oh, that's just who I'd want on my side in all of this, a man everyone on the lake calls weird!" my dad groaned sarcastically.

"Wait a minute, have you been talking to him!?" My mom asked sharply, her eyes swelling. "What did I tell you about him? Don't tell me you don't remember my warning!"

"People call him weird because his family has millions and yet his cottage is the most run down on the lake," I groaned. "He has a creepy way of staring at people and has worn the same dungarees, lumberjack shirt, and white bucket hat since you and Dad were both kids.

He's the only one who lives on the lake all year, and yet hasn't had any visitors, ever. He's never left his property and he practices absolutely no type of personal hygiene whatso-ever. He's lived his whole life on a lake, and yet nobody has ever seen him go into the water. He never turns on any lights inside his cottage at night and the only upgrade he's ever made to his property is buying new KEEP OUT signs every year. He eats cold beans from a can with his hands and on the Fourth of July he always—"

"That's enough," Mom interrupted. "You know all of this, yet you still trust what he has to say?"

"Leave Harold out of this," Dad ordered, training his still-buttered knife on me. "Quit listening to him, quit talking to him, and quit calling him weird. One of these days you're going to call him Weird Harold to his face by accident, then what!?"

"Then he'll know we think he's weird?" Kyle answered.

"The idea of any neighbor, let alone one who has known you for all of two days now, wanting to kill you is completely insane," Dad explained.

"Don't you think it's the least bit strange that Art has been around every time one of these freak accidents has hap-pened?" I asked. "What are the odds?"

"He's our neighbor, Kay. If your neighbors weren't around most of the time then they wouldn't be your neighbors!" My father offered, explaining the obvious as only he could.

"Exactly, Art's our neighbor!" I roared. "That means he could have easily sawed the limb on the tree or rigged the garage door to fall."

Dad didn't answer. Instead, his head shook back and forth like a bobblehead doll, that vein tripling in size. He bit viciously into his French bread and chewed until his mouth was so full his cheeks looked like each contained a softball. Clearly he was through arguing.

"You know, now that you mention it, I thought I heard somebody snooping around in our shed last night," Kyle announced unexpectedly. "I never thought it might have been the Big A."

"All right listen!" Dad erupted, shards of French bread exploding from his mouth. "I'm not going to sit around for the rest of the week listening to you people spinning some ridiculous theory about a neighbor trying to kill you!" A hush fell over the table. "This might be our last week on the lake. We shouldn't waste it trying to send our neighbor to jail! Let's just clean this mess up and get to bed. When the sun comes up tomorrow, we're going to forget all about this nonsense and we're going to ride around the lake and waterski and do things families do on vacations; things like have fun, run around in the sun, and enjoy ourselves! And if anyone mentions Art Guilafante *or* Weird Harold *or* calls me Walter again, I'll throw them overboard!"

"I thought we weren't supposed to call him weird," Abby fired back.

"Another question like that and you'll be treading water for six hours in the sun, young lady."

"That should lock up the father of the year award for sure! That is, if they don't lock you up for a year first!" I snapped.

"Zip it, Kay. Or the two of you will be treading water together!"

Before I could respond, a loud noise came crashing through the window. "What was *that?*" Kyle asked.

My mind leapt to Art Guilafante. Was he snooping around? Was he out plotting another accident? My heart stopped.

"There's something outside," Dad announced, dealing in the obvious once again.

We all headed for the back door in a group. Strength in numbers wasn't something I had subscribed to until Art Guilafante had moved in next door. Hiding in the shadows we found the lid to our trash can on the ground. "What the heck?" Dad muttered under his breath.

That's when I spotted Tricky's bushy tail dangling out of the can.

"Is that…?" Before I could finish my thought, Dad had grabbed a baseball bat from the corner of the shed.

He took a hard swing at the can's side. He looked like Kyle jumping on my fastball. In one swift motion, my dad sent the can, Tricky, and all of our garbage tumbling over. Undeterred, the raccoon righted himself and climbed back inside the can, eager for more.

Dad seethed, his face red with rage. What came next were multiple slams of the bat off the can and a series of words I'm not allowed to repeat. By the time he was done, my dad had sent Tricky, the trash can, and most of our garbage screaming down the driveway as if each had been shot from a cannon. Watermelon rinds and potato peelings were strewn everywhere. Our driveway had become a mural of used Kleenex and paper plates stained red with lasagna. The raccoon righted himself in time to see my dad, angry and barefoot, racing through the trash after him on tiptoes. Understandably, the sight of the bat made Tricky nervous.

But before Dad could get to the little menace, he slipped on an empty potato chip bag and fell backwards onto a carton of expired milk. The force of his weight caused the carton to explode, coating him in spoiled milk. I closed my eyes in shame.

As Dad lay in the trash cursing, Tricky bounced away into the shadows leaving behind a driveway full of garbage.

From the safety of his redwood fence, Harold Farcus was looking on. Surely, somewhere beneath that white bucket hat, a tiny giggle lurked. Meanwhile, Tricky the make-up wearing, trash-eating raccoon, disappeared into the night in search of more garbage cans.

11

~~~~~~~

B etween dive bombing floatplanes and collapsing garage doors and the faulty rope swing, the lake was turning out to be a dangerous place after all. Part of me was starting to believe Art Guilafante and his warnings about old places. This same part of me was close to asking my parents to leave the lake.

The tiny voice in my head was saying the only way my family could survive the week was to pack up and go home. Thankfully, I was really good at ignoring it, so I lit out once again for the swamp.

The far side of the lake was starting to take on a new meaning. It seemed the only place Art Guilafante had yet to try getting his meaty paws on me. It was also the only place I'd been all week without bumping into him, and the only place I'd been where I hadn't almost died.

Grandpa's notes about the ibis showed just how close he'd been for so many years. 'May 18, 1985-Heard a pair grunting' and 'July 22, 1991-Single ibis calling at dusk from west side of swamp', but there was no check mark.

Grandpa was always telling me how Teddy Roosevelt could identify a bird quicker by song than sight, but Grandpa was a 'gotta see it to believe it' kind of guy and only checked a bird off in his book when he had actually seen it. The book was full of them. There were one hundred and ninety seven total, but the glossy ibis was one of the few that was missing. If I had my way, I was about to fix that.

I knew my best chance was finding a stray nesting with some herons, but settling in on a nest would be done later in the day, so my plan involved hugging the bank to look for signs of one probing the mud for insects. This would at least tell me if any were around.

The swamp was quiet. I stepped through the switch grass and clumps of wild oats to stop near a stand of sycamores. A nearby button bush filled the air with its sweet scent as I watched a wood thrush darting from one branch to the other. He lit a few feet away. Twitching his tail nervously, he aimed one of his large round eyes in my direction.

Then something else caught my eye. A bright flash just ahead. Could it be the iridescent wings of the glossy ibis? My heart surged. A few careful steps forward led me to a bulrush near the edge of the water.

That's when I saw her. Long and lean and chattering her way through the swamp. It wasn't a female ibis; it was the Trash Queen. And she was singing, again. "Hush a bye, don't you cry, go to sleep little baby, when you awake, you shall have all the pretty horses."

Her voice was wobbly and off key, which made her singing sound like someone stepping on a cat. I was never going to find a glossy ibis with this lady around. "Agnes?" I spoke softly, in the hopes my words might bring her singing to an end. There was no response. The Trash Queen kept singing and dancing around as if she were on Broadway. "Agnes?" I shouted in a whisper.

"Who is it?" she asked, spinning around. "Why, it's my little birder! Hello there dearie." She greeted loudly, as if a football field separated us instead of a few feet. "What brings you to the swamp today? On the hunt for your ibis again?"

"Yes," I answered, making no effort to mask my annoyance. "What are you doing here?"

Agnes shifted her sun hat before holding up a basket of wildflowers. "The phlox is just too beautiful right now. I simply must have some at home, and my poor husband Charlie…gets poison ivy so bad this time of year, jewel weed is the only thing that'll clear it up." Agnes pulled her sunglasses down past the bridge of her nose to stare at the Band-Aids on my forehead, temporary tattoos left behind by my wrestling match with the falling garage door. "What happened to your face, dearie?"

"Oh nothing. A shed door just fell on my brother and me, that's all."

A strange look washed over the Trash Queen's face. For a moment she appeared ready to ask about the door before quickly deciding some stones were best left unturned, "Well, what about that ibis of yours, dearie? Any luck?"

The sun lit up the roses stitched into the breast of her denim vest. She was something to behold. Bright yellow shorts and a denim top, pink floppy sunhat, and her feet clomping around in those same clumsy storm boots she'd had on the last time I'd seen her.

"Not yet," I answered. That part of me, the one I'd grown so used to ignoring, was telling me to ask Agnes to leave the swamp and never come back. The way she was beaming and dancing around, it seemed she was absolutely clueless to the fact that her singing was a major hurdle between me and a glossy ibis.

I searched for the most polite words I could find. 'Please, Agnes, could you do me a favor and leave the swamp forever?' seemed a bit strong, while 'Don't take this personally Agnes, but I really don't want you here right now', didn't seem to have the right ring to it either.

"What about that grandfather of yours, dearie? Where's he at today?"

The question hit me like a punch in the stomach. It stung me harder than a Roni Bonafetti dodgeball. Almost immediately, the Trash Queen's words made the world stop. The colors of the swamp faded to gray. The sounds of the chittering birds and rustling sycamores fell silent.

My mind leapfrogged from the bench on the pier to the seat in Grandpa's Toy to Grandpa Tug's place at the dinner table. They were all empty now. They'd been empty ever since we came back. Grandpa Tug really was gone.

It hadn't fully hit me until that moment. Standing in the swamp staring at the Trash Queen fussing over her wildflowers. It was an innocent question, but one that rocked me to the core. My Grandpa Tug wasn't coming back. Ever.

Every day for the last two years I'd woke up fully expecting him to call me on the phone or stop by the house. A small part of me, the part I typically listened to most, said he'd be waiting for me at the lake. Somehow I'd fooled myself into believing that he'd been up here for the last two years, roaming the swamp and hanging out with Harold while waiting for me to come back, but now it was clear. Grandpa Tug was gone.

I wasn't ready to let go. Grandpa was everything to me. There were still so many things I wanted to say to him and do with him. But all that was gone now and the world seemed very strange, as if Grandpa hadn't taught me a thing. I didn't recognize anything around me. Trees and grasses I once knew by heart seemed so foreign now.

Suddenly the swamp was full of dangerous things; insects longing to bite you and transfer diseases from their bloodstream to yours, putrid water that held so much bacteria it would take a team of doctors from around the world to find all the cures and, not to mention, foul-tempered raccoons possessing razor sharp teeth, powerful claws, and the rabies virus. What was I doing here?

"Is everything all right, dearie?" Agnes asked, raising a hand to my shoulder softly.

The touch seemed to bring color back to the swamp. The chittering of birds and sound of the wind through the trees rushed back. For the first time I saw the Trash Queen's eyes, blue as a summer sky. They were filled with compassion. That's when it hit me. I realized then what I'd seen in Agnes the last time. She was just like my Grandma Minnie, always so loud about everything she did and yet, just when you needed it most, always ready to lend an ear.

Like the silver maples and Grandpa Tug and myself, Agnes was a fellow guardian of the swamp. Feeling I could trust her now, I told Agnes everything: how Grandpa Tug was the greatest man I knew. How he built his cottage and taught pretty much everybody on the lake, and the history of the world for that matter, to water ski. How he'd conducted his own bird counts in the swamp every year since forever. I told her how he could identify thirty different birds just by hearing their calls and how the call of the screech owl was always our favorite. I also told the Trash Queen Grandpa Tug was gone.

"I'm sorry, dearie, I didn't realize that. He sounds like such an incredible man."

"I just really thought he would be here. He'd been sick for two years. I mean everybody knew it wasn't good. I don't know. Somehow I just thought he was out here all along, taking counts and making notes. I mean, I went to the funeral. I saw him there, but somehow it wasn't real."

The sky opened up as a shaft of light fell on Agnes, making it appear as if she were glowing. A golden statue rising from the jewel weed and clover. For a moment she didn't speak. It was just the two of us surrounded by the noise of the swamp. "I know what you're saying, sweetie, but just think of the amazing memories he left you with! You know, just like that bird book there, your brain is full of incredible experiences you shared with your grandpa. He may be gone now, but it doesn't matter what happens. Memories are forever, my dearie. Nobody can take them away from you."

I was glad I hadn't kicked Agnes out of my swamp. She was a kind person. It had been there all along, and I had missed it. She cared for the swamp, serving as a guardian while I was gone. She cared for the birds and the wildlife and she cared for her husband Charlie. "I'll tell you something else, dearie," she said, a gleam filling her eye. "Your grandpa was a very smart man. He taught you to love this place because he knew someday he wouldn't be around. Sure, he hid it from you, but he could rest safe in the knowledge that when his time came, there would always be somebody around to protect this place."

The words hit me hard. All those years spent exploring the swamp, noting the plants, counting birds. All those years had been more than just a grandfather spending time with his granddaughter. All those years he'd been preparing me. Preparing me for this moment. The day had finally come for me to pick up where he left off. It was my job to protect the swamp now, and there was no way I was going to let my Grandpa Tug down.

12
~~~~~~~

The Big A's shed was dark. My trembling hand wandered along the wall desperately seeking a light switch. I wasn't sure how I'd gotten here. In fact, this was the last place on Earth I wanted to be.

My first and only real conversation with Weird Harold Farcus had led to the maybe not so brilliant idea of snooping through Art's garage. Harold had said if Art was hiding anything, we'd find it there. One five minute discussion with a man who smelled of rotting fish and musty taxidermy, and suddenly I was a detective.

It took me about three seconds to realize I didn't even know what I was looking for. In fact, I didn't know the first thing about being a detective. The ones on TV made it look so simple. Interview a couple people, find something in a dumpster and bingo, you've solved a mystery. This wasn't about being a detective. It was more about a suggestion Weird Harold had made. This was also about protecting the swamp. Agnes had been right, all this time I'd been waiting on Grandpa to come back and take care of everything when he'd already taught me to do it on my own.

"What are we looking for?" Kyle whispered.

"Right now a light switch," I answered honestly.

Art and his family had gone in to town. That meant they'd be gone for at least a half hour or more. Time wasn't an issue, so outside of the fact I was basically entering someone else's garage illegally, and my parents would likely disown me for doing so, there was no reason to be nervous- yet something told me Art's shed was a dangerous place. There was even a good chance it was booby trapped. Art wasn't stupid. Harold had said so himself.

Everything ran back to Grandpa Tug. That day he'd tried teaching me to ski. We were back in the water, Grandpa's Toy gurgling softly as Grandpa stood by my side in waist deep water. He could feel me trembling. "You can't spend your whole life running away from the things you're scared of," he whispered in my ear.

I'd heard that line before. In fact, the first time Grandpa used it Kyle asked if it was okay to run away from the Abominable Snow Monster from the North. "You know, the one that tried to eat Rudolph?" He had squealed.

When Grandpa nodded, Dad slid the boat into gear. The rope drew tight in my hands and started pulling me through the water. Grandpa was sure to keep a hand on my jacket as long as he could. Those giant skis were so hard to keep together. I could still hear Grandpa's voice yelling, "Sit on the chair! Sit on the chair!"

Outside the faint sound of a ski boat on the lake could be heard. The inside of Art's shed felt like an oven. The air was stuffy and thick, pitch black, yet I could sense things around me: boxes, buckets and random other things people didn't need but refused to toss out. Still, I didn't know what I was looking for. I didn't know anything about solving crimes.

I knew about animals. Things like how muskrats can stay underwater for almost twenty minutes, and the scientific name for a raccoon is *lotor*, which means 'washer' even though they don't really 'wash' their food in the sense that we humans do. I knew that a kingfisher, just like an owl, spits up pellets of bone and undigested material, and that a woodchuck sounds an alarm when he's scared that sounds just like a whistle, which is why some call him a whistle pig.

The dull sound of Kyle running into something filled the shed. "Keep it down!" I whispered. "We're not supposed to be in here, remember?"

"Sorry, it's just I'm not that good at running an obstacle course of junk in the dark. I thought Harold said a storm knocked Jimmy's shed down anyway?"

"It crushed part of it. Besides, Art does run what's called a construction company, remember? Now quit asking questions and keep looking."

Harold said we needed to find something that would prove Art was trying to hurt us. Something that told us Art was doing more than just building condos on the lake. Harold called it a smoking gun. Maybe finding one wouldn't be that hard. Maybe there would be a handsaw or an axe just lying around. Maybe we'd be able to get the Big A's fingerprints off of it just like the real TV detectives do.

If we were really lucky, I thought we might find a checklist of all the ways Art planned on killing us, or at the very least a copy of 'The Idiot's Guide to Killing Your Neighbor' with all the parts about the best methods for sawing tree limbs and garage door supports highlighted.

"Ow!" Kyle shrieked.

"What happened?"

"I don't know, I think I stepped on a knife or something. Whatever it was went right through my shoe."

I found the light switch and flipped it. A single bare bulb overhead came to life. A sea of random things appeared before me. A few cardboard boxes, some empty plastic buckets, a pile of rusted lawn chairs, an old shovel lying on the floor and a pair of wooden water skis that were holding down a tangled up garden hose.

"What was it?"

"Looks like a drill. Who just leaves a drill lying in the floor of their shed? Especially one with a razor sharp bit on it? I'm lucky the thing only gashed my shoe and not my foot!"

"I don't know, but be more careful," I said, glancing at the drill. "You're making too much noise!"

Looking at all the stuff surrounding us, a strange feeling began to creep over me. This was more than just stuff; it was Art Guilafante's stuff. Something told me we shouldn't be here. It was that same voice that told me not to confront Art during the barbecue, and I had a really bad habit of ignoring its perceptible wisdom, especially considering we'd crossed over into new territory. The whole idea of entering somebody else's shed just felt wrong. In fact, I hadn't felt this way since Alison Camarillo asked to copy my math homework in fifth grade. I knew it wasn't the right thing to do, but I let her anyway because she was my best friend.

"What are we looking for again?" Kyle asked.

"A smoking gun."

Kyle stopped to look at the sea of junk surrounding us. "You mean like James Bond's Walther PPK?"

I didn't have time to wade through one of Kyle's obscure movie references. We had to find something and get out of the shed as fast as we could. Time was wasting. I began flipping boxes open. One was full of old clothes, another of old books and old magazines. One had old dishes in it, and then another full of a lot more old magazines.

As I let the flap of the box drop, something caught my eye. It was an address label on a faded copy of *Field and Stream*. It said James Strabobbi. 'James' as in Jimmy? Jimmy as in Jimmy Longstockings? Could it be? Did all this all stuff belong to Jimmy Longstockings? A strange thought brewed quickly in my stomach. Slowly it began to crawl up my spine, tingling its way toward my brain. Once in my head, the thought began shouting at the top of its lungs.

"Kyle, look at this." I said, picking one of the magazines up.

"James Strabobbi." Kyle read the name aloud.

"Do you know what this means?"

"The magazine got delivered to the wrong person?"

"Remember how Harold said Jimmy left in a hurry after the tree fell? I think all these boxes belong to Jimmy. Even if he did leave in a hurry, would he really leave this much stuff behind?"

"Wait a minute," Kyle said, reaching for the power button on his camera. "I've got to get this. This would be a tremendous shot for the climax of *The Curse of Bass Lake*."

If Jimmy planned on moving away, why would he leave all his stuff behind? Who would do something like that? I remembered when Alison Camarillo moved away. There were two trucks outside her house for an entire day loading one box after another after another. When the Camarillo's left, nothing, absolutely nothing was left behind but an empty house.

I guess I only remembered that because I was convinced the only reason Alison was moving was because she knew someone was after us for cheating on our math homework. Her family had decided they needed to get out of town fast before the cops caught up with us. Despite this, I was sure nobody would move away from their home and leave this much stuff behind. Something strange was definitely going on here.

With Kyle's camera humming, I reached my hand down to look for more stuff. Before I could grab another magazine, a noise was heard outside. Footsteps. Big...heavy...plodding footsteps, the kind that could only belong to Art Guilafante.

"Hurry up! Hide!"

The sound of the shoes crunching through the gravel was getting louder. I scrambled to the wall and flipped the light switch off before diving behind a pile of boxes where I was sure to be out of sight. The sounds of Kyle clumsily ducking himself into the corner of the shed bounced off the walls.

Then a large shadow flashed across the wall as someone stepped into the doorway. The shadow itself was nearly ten feet in length. My chest heaved. My throat turned dry, as if I'd swallowed a spoonful of sand.

Through a crack between the boxes I watched a pair of shoes step into the shed. Could Art be back from town already? Maybe something had brought him back. I guessed it was something along the lines of he'd forgotten his sunglasses or the fact he hadn't killed me yet. The feet shuffled back and forth in front of me for a moment. Then they stopped. They were pointed straight at me. Whoever they belonged to was looking right at me.

This was not good. My heart began pounding harder, as if looking for the quickest way out of my chest, the quickest way out of the shed for that matter. I could only imagine what Art would do if he found me here, snooping around.

He would probably pound me flat as a pancake and toss me across the lake like a human Frisbee.

The feet shifted one way then the other. Whoever this was appeared to be looking for something. Was it me? Then they took a step straight at me. I watched as two hands reached down and pushed the boxes apart.

I threw my hands up over my head quickly to protect myself. This was it. My life was over. Over before my thirteenth birthday. Over before I could find a glossy ibis. Over before I'd even had a chance to get revenge on Roni Bonafetti. Over before I could fully admit to the crime of allowing Alison Camarillo to copy my math homework.

"Kayla?" thundered a deep voice. "What are *you* doing in here!?"

13

~~~~~~~

I didn't answer right away. Instead, I just sat there ignoring the question as if I'd been born without ears.

"Why are you in Art's shed?" My dad asked, reaching down to grab me by the arm.

I don't know how to explain what happened next because I don't even know where the idea came from. Maybe it was a reflex. Maybe it was the hand of Grandpa Tug himself reaching down to give me the single greatest alibi in the history of snoopers caught snooping. Either way, what came from my mouth next was nothing short of solid gold.

"Kyle and I were playing hide and seek. I figured he'd never find me in here!"

"Kayla Marie! You don't go around playing in other people's houses and sheds. This place doesn't belong to us! It belongs to Art!"

Dad had explained this last part as if he truly thought I was a complete imbecile. Of course, I was fine with this at that moment. This far outweighed the alternative which likely involved my joining a convent or worse yet, mowing the yard by myself for the next sixty years.

"You shouldn't be in here. Get out, now!" He shouted in a whisper, pointing a finger toward the door.

"Okay, okay." I said, pulling my arm loose to leave.

For a moment it looked like I was going to get away with snooping in Art's shed. Two more steps and I would have been out the door, but just as I was almost home free, the sound of clanging metal rang out from behind me. My dad's attention darted toward the sound. That's when the patio umbrella Kyle was hiding behind fell over to the floor.

"Kyle?" my dad yelled. "Why are you in here too?"

The vein in Dad's head was beginning to swell. It was already halfway to atomic, and I knew atomic. I'd seen atomic the day Kyle brought our pet hamster, Dingy, to church. It wasn't Dingy's first trip to church, but it was the first time he gnawed a hole in Kyle's pocket and raced down the inside of his pant leg before getting loose. Sure Kyle tried to get him back. He scrambled around under the pews trying to grab him, trying to hide the fact a rodent was loose in church. Of course, it's a pretty obvious sign something is wrong when someone is crawling around under the pews during church.

Dingy made his way to the front much faster than I even thought possible. Normally most might not have noticed, but on this Sunday people were busy trudging back and forth taking communion. As dumb luck would have it, Dingy found his way under the feet of the only ninety-five-year-old woman in our church.

Dad offered to replace the widow Gerka's hip, but she was a true God-fearing woman who knew that Dingy had found her for a reason. Still, that vein on Dad's head didn't relax for almost a full week.

Now Kyle stood with a confused look on his face. "Kyle, I asked why you were in Art's shed."

Most people think twins have ESP or the ability to talk to each other without actually speaking. My experience tells me that's hogwash, but at that moment I was willing to try anything. I bent my brow and tried my hardest to throw some words into my brother's cavernous brain. 'We were playing hide and seek'. That was all he had to say. 'We were playing hide and seek'. If Kyle would just say, 'We were playing hide and seek', Dad would walk away and the whole thing would be forgotten.

"We were looking for a smoking gun," Kyle finally answered.

"A smoking what?" Dad repeated.

Suddenly there it was again. That tiny voice I really needed to learn to ignore. "Dad," I asked, turning back to him from the doorway, "What are *you* doing in here?"

My dad's face bent in confusion. I hoped to switch him from offense to defense. "Art said I could borrow a shovel, but that doesn't change the fact that you were in here without his permission!" Dad's barking caused the vein to swell even more.

Now here we were. The four of us alone in Art Guilafante's shed. Kyle, me, my dad and that creepy vein on his forehead. "If you were playing hide and seek, why were you both hiding? Wait a minute. Does this have something to do with all that nonsense you were saying at dinner the other night? About Art wanting to hurt you? Is that why you're in here?"

I froze. Where to begin? I couldn't possibly tell him that this had all been Harold's idea because that would open a whole new, 'Why have you been talking to Weird Harold when we clearly told you not to?' can of worms. A few old magazines and dishes wouldn't be enough to pass muster as evidence. The only thing I had going for me was our teaming up with Weird Harold, and at least my parents didn't know anything about that.

Then Kyle opened the can himself. "It was all Harold's idea, Dad," Kyle confessed on his way to the door.

My dad's face burned for a moment. "You know what, I don't even want to know what you're talking about right now," He said thumbing at the door. "Just get out already."

"But, Dad…" I stalled, trying to bring his attention to the plethora of clues surrounding him.

I couldn't connect the dots yet, but maybe Dad could. If only he would notice on his own. Then maybe it wouldn't seem like such a wild idea that our neighbor was trying to get rid of us. "No buts, Kayla. You two are coming with me. Looks like we need to have a talk with your mother."

As Dad led the way to our cottage, I couldn't keep myself from kicking my brother hard in the shin.

"OWW! What was that for!?" There was no time to explain. The trial of Kayla and Kyle Minnix was about to begin.

14
~~~~~~~

The trial hadn't lasted long, and from what I'd seen on TV, it wasn't much of a trial at all. I never even got a chance to speak, which I'm pretty sure was a violation of my rights as an American. It was just Mom and Dad yelling at my brother and me about personal space and personal property and a bunch of other stuff they had probably kept bottled up for a while. Dad's vein was there too, looking more enlarged and upset than ever.

The unsettling turn of events that came from the trial was that somehow, somebody had come up with the worst punishment ever. Dad said it would be 'simple', and while 'simple' was the word they chose, I didn't see how it fit at all. 'Dangerous' seemed more appropriate to me. Either way, one thing was clear. We had to apologize to Art Guilafante.

After all that had happened, they were going to send us marching off into the arms of the enemy, practically forcing us to surrender. I might as well go wearing a shirt that said 'Kill me now' or 'My parents no longer care about my health and safety; you may now take me from this world'.

With Ella standing guard from a nearby branch, Bud worked hard packing mud along the overhang of Art Guilafante's cottage. His purple feathers glowed blue under the bright sun as he flitted about, bringing small daubs back from the lake one at a time.

From the comfort of Grandpa Tug's hammock, I watched the pair building their dream home. At that moment, theirs seemed such a carefree world. There were no planes trying to fly into the side of their nest, and nobody was out to destroy all that was sacred to them. I wanted to be in that world, though I knew it wasn't possible.

I tried to forget everything Weird Harold had said. How Jimmy's dog had disappeared and how that old tree had almost crushed him while he slept. How Harold had never seen the limb of a maple crack so easily, or how nobody could build a shed stronger than my Grandpa Tug.

I couldn't shake the image of the Big A and his hacksaw. His big voice filled my head, his ominous words bouncing back and forth, 'Everything has a price tag…someone could get hurt *real* bad'. How was I supposed to apologize to this guy? I mean just how do you apologize to a monster, after all?

Still, my parents were absolutely convinced Art Guilafante didn't want to hurt us. Maybe this was all part of my imagination after all. Maybe Art was just an ordinary neighbor who just happened to be around after every accident I'd survived.

Ella paced back and forth anxiously, as if telling Bud to work faster. Ever the soldier, Bud kept at it while the nest began to take shape. I imagined the clutch of eggs Ella would soon hatch. I could see little Bud puffing out his chest while showing his young brood how to hunt around the lake.

"Hey look!" Kyle shouted, pointing down Lake Road, "Here comes Mom!"

Edging around the curve we saw Mom coming with the boat trailer in tow. "That means Dad's on his way. Let's go!" In a blur, Kyle raced by and slapped me on the back of the head.

I knew exactly where he was going, so I tumbled out of the hammock to beat him there. Grandpa Tug loved the far side of the lake so much that he built a lookout tower behind his cottage where he could have a better view of everything. As we'd done a hundred times before, Kyle and I raced each other up the exterior set of stairs spiraling our way to the top. Kyle worked the door open and we climbed inside. The plastic windows muffled the noise of the lake as Kyle struggled to get his camera ready.

"Why didn't I think about a panoramic shot earlier?" he whined, training his camera on the lake which was spread out before us.

I picked up Grandpa's old field glasses and quickly drew them into focus, following the quiet ring of A-shaped cottages until they ended on the far side of the lake. Where the cottages stopped, the construction began. Giant, three story condominiums towered above the shoreline. The unfinished condos, with their white paper siding, might as well have been giant silver disks from Mars. Either way, they didn't belong on Grandpa Tug's Bass Lake. On a shoreline dotted with maples and birch trees, the apartment complex seemed oddly misplaced, a child's toy carelessly left behind. The hair on the back of my neck bristled.

I watched big ugly bulldozers pushing the soil around, farting dark clouds of black smoke. In my mind I could see Art on the beach, bullhorn in hand. Unhappy with the progress, he was demanding his men work faster, all the while screaming, "Beaches don't make money!"

The words and the man sent my stomach tumbling. He'd told us this was happening, but I hadn't seen it until now. The construction workers scurried about like an army of ants in blue jeans and hardhats. Giant trucks roared to and fro, their plumes of exhaust smoke filling the sky with a coal colored haze. Backhoes were busy uprooting trees as if pulling weeds in a flowerbed.

Then I saw them, the shorebirds. Creatures that should be left to explore the edge of the lake were now helpless, frantically scrambling from the paths of steamrollers. The whole scene was utterly terrifying. 'Nothing stays the same anymore,' Weird Harold's voice echoed through my head.

"Just look at that action, Kay. It's natural. It's real. It's authentic. That was a scene made for the big screen!"

The lake was full of sun faded runabouts twisting and turning in all directions. A flashy new wakeboard boat raced across the water. This oversized beast wore a flamboyant aluminum tower that looked more like a tiara.

I gnashed my teeth over the thought of those birds being run from their homes. "Who will save the shore birds?" I muttered aloud.

"There's Dad!" Kyle gasped, pointing.

I dialed the goggles in on the boats and found Grandpa's Toy, my father at the wheel with the wind rippling his hair. The old wood boat bounced effortlessly through the whiteheads on her way toward our cottage. The honey brown hull cut through rippling whitecaps as a bright American flag flew proudly from her stern.

"Come on, let's go down to the dock!" Kyle chortled. "I want to get a shot of Dad pulling up to the pier."

I set the goggles on the sill and scrambled through the hole in the lookout floor. Together our feet began racing down the steps. Halfway down, the pounding of our shoes was soon replaced by a massive groan. Suddenly the tower jolted violently as it tore loose from the cottage. I scrabbled for something to hold on to as we began teetering. For one beautiful moment that old lookout hung in the air, leaning like that one famous tower in Italy. The one you see on almost every pizza box ever made. In that moment, Kyle turned to me. When our eyes met, we both knew what the other was thinking. But before we could speak, the moment was over and the lookout promptly tumbled to the ground like a giant bowling pin.

The collapse caused the ground to judder. The planks of the stairway exploded in all directions. That old lookout, which had stood for nearly fifty years, collapsed in less than five seconds. Now it was a pile of rubble that looked less like a lookout and more like a circus elephant had sat on an Adirondack chair.

"What now!?" Abby shrieked, racing around the side of the cottage.

When she found us lying amidst a pile of broken steps and busted supports, she lost it.

"Oh my God! Mom is going to kill me! All you had to do was keep it together while she ran Dad to the marina and *now* look what you've done!!" Expressing, in true teenager fashion, Abby's complete concern for herself.

Thankfully, the cabin at the top of the lookout had missed us. The weight of this alone would have been enough to crush us like ladybugs under a steel toed boot.

"You guys okay?" Another voice asked upon arriving at the scene. There it was again. That same big, dumb voice I was growing all too familiar with.

Was this really happening again? Art Guilafante showing up to offer another so-called '*rescue*'? "We're fine," I answered from beneath the tangle of split boards and shattered stairs. "Just playing in the lookout tower, that's all."

Clearly I wasn't fine. Fine is building a castle out of sand on the beach under a blazing hot summer sun. Fine is coming in from sledding in the snow to find a steaming mug of hot cocoa waiting for you on the kitchen table. I'd almost been killed for the fourth time in five days, which meant I was about as far from fine as you could possibly be. But at that moment I didn't want to give Art any reasons to hang around.

"I guess there's no sense telling your dad he should tear this thing down. You did that for him!" Art said, tossing pieces of wood aside quickly until I could sit up again.

"Goodness gracious, what's happened now!?" My mom cried out, racing over from the driveway.

"The lookout collapsed," Art explained.

He spoke the words slowly, as if my mom wouldn't be able to put that together on her own. "You're lucky this chimbley didn't come down too," the Big A added, running his hands over the brick of a nearby chimney.

Chimbley? I hadn't come across the world chimbley since I'd read *How the Grinch Stole Christmas*. Now, standing there looking down at me, Art Guilafante seemed to change. The evil gleam in his eye, the crooked grin on his face. Suddenly he looked more like a devious, paunchy green monster bent on stealing Christmas than the rakish, athletic man he was.

"The weight of that alone would have been enough to have crushed every bone in your body," observed Art.

My eyes darted to Mom. Had she heard that? There Art was again, talking about something killing her children.

"I'll have some of the guys from the construction site come over tonight and clear this mess out of here," the Big A offered.

Construction workers? At the lake cottage? That was the last thing we needed. Bulldozers, backhoes, and dump trucks taller than two story houses? Nobody wanted those mechanical monsters over here.

"Thanks, Art, but you've already done enough just being here." Mom responded, still in shock. The look on her face told me the forced apology she'd asked us to give was nowhere on her radar now.

"Suit yourself...but you gotta watch these old places, Kathy. They can be really dangerous sometimes. Especially if someone hasn't used it for a long time," Art Guilafante warned, giving the cottage a once over with his big eyes, "It's just a real miracle everyone survived."

Art winked at my mom when he was done. There it was again. That wink never failed to chill my spine. He wasn't glad anyone had survived. What a creep. I stared him down as he rose and strode away slowly.

"You're on some kind of unbelievable streak of bad luck!" Mom offered, checking my forehead for cuts.

"It's more than unbelievable, Mom," I answered when the Big A was out of earshot. "It's too strange to be true."

From behind the safety of his redwood fence, I saw Harold Farcus. He had watched the whole thing. I found a faint look of worry leaking out from under his white bucket hat. It was clear Harold and I had the same concerns; Big Art Guilafante's plans didn't stop at the far side of the lake.

From his Too-Big-for-Bass-Lake-Floatplane to his Too-Big-for-Bass-Lake-Bluster, the Big A had big plans for

Bass Lake. Art Guilafante always got whatever he wanted. It was clear that Jimmy Longstockings had been persuaded to get out of Art's way, and now we were next.

15

~~~~~~~

B elted kingfishers are as powerful as they are striking. They tend to look like a hummingbird with a hammer on their head. A wild tuft of hair streaking backwards from his crown makes it look like something from a cartoon, but this is soon forgotten when you see one diving for a fish.

Wilbert Harley wasn't nearly as striking as a belted kingfisher. He was short, bald, and had a handlebar mustache that had gone out of style when William Howard Taft left the White House. Still, no matter his appearance, Wilbert Harley did have one thing going for him; he was President of the Lake.

Of course he really wasn't President of the Lake, rather Harley was President of the Lake Owners Association. His card also said he was Second Vice President of the California County Gourd Growers Society, as if that somehow lent him more political credibility.

"My name's President Wilbert Harley!" The man beamed brightly while ramming his pudgy hand into my sister's. "Glad to meet ya!"

"The President? Really?" Abby answered, her face beaming with excitement. "This is wild! Where's the Secret

Service at?" She glanced around the empty yard behind the man.

I felt like introducing her as the Queen of Hormonestan but was worried that would only bring more confusion to an already awkward situation. "Oh, is that an agent in that tree up there?" the Queen asked in a whisper.

"No, Abby, that's a squirrel's nest," I clarified.

Wilbert Harley gave my sister a strange look before continuing, "Well, isn't it wonderful weather we've been having? Another beauteous day on Bass Lake!"

He looked just like those crusty old presidents from the back of your history book, only he was wearing cargo shorts and Jesus sandals. His round figure and thick mustache made him seem closer to Harding or Taft, whichever one got stuck in the bathtub.

The President's deep tan also made him look like an older, more wrinkled version of Mr. Potato head. And, judging by his generous belly, I decided the only thing President Potato-Head had ever really debated was which pizza topping to order.

"Your parents around?" he asked, tugging a handkerchief across his sweaty, gourd shaped head.

"No, they needed to take a walk," I answered.

"Too bad! I was really hoping to catch up with them today. How'r things on this side of the lake anyway?" With Kyle, Abby and I blocking the door, the President's eyes were trying their best to pry their way inside our cottage. "I don't get over to this side much."

Judging by his waistline, I found myself thinking the President didn't get anywhere very much. "Things are fine," Abby answered quickly.

Maybe things were fine in Hormonestan, but here in the real world, things were most definitely not fine. I guess she believed things were fine only because it had been me that had almost died four times, not her.

"Well, they're a busy batch of beavers on the far side of the lake; got a set of condos going up, all kinds of construction trucks running back and forth everywhere- just noisy as a henhouse full of foxes."

"Sounds grand," I snorted sarcastically.

"You can't stop progress," Wilbert Harley explained. "Yessiree, we've gone far too long on this lake without some changes. It's about time we shook things up around here."

Nobody responded. I couldn't tell if the President was smart enough to realize none of us agreed with him or if he was just really bad at making conversation. "Feels good to find some quiet over here, though," he admitted.

"I'll bet the herons would appreciate some quiet on the far side of the lake. Did you know there are rookeries near the construction site? And mallard nests too?" I asked.

The President didn't respond. I could only assume he cared so little for the birds because herons and mallards weren't registered to vote in California County.

"Anyway, I was sure sorry to hear about your grandpa," the President admitted. "Old Tug and I, we were some of the first property owners up here. Well, us and Harold's father, Weed, of course." The man finished, nodding toward the white bucket hat staring at us from behind that redwood fence.

"That's Weird Harold," Kyle announced in a whisper. All eyes fell on Harold, who was holding Larry in his arms, stroking him like cat. "My dad says we're not supposed to call him weird…" Kyle's eyes danced as he finished, "apparently he doesn't know he's weird, so let's just keep that between us, okay?"

The President didn't respond. Instead his wide eyes took a trip up and down Kyle's legs, exploring the maze of

Band Aids where the falling lookout had chewed them up worse than an angry Beaver. This sparked a confused look in the man's eyes as he went on, "Your grandfather was the nicest man I ever knew. And boy, could he ski like no one else!"

"Really?" Kyle asked.

"Oh yeah, two skis, slalom, trick skis, barefoot. Heck once I even saw him ski on a ladder!"

"Ski on a ladder!?" Abby snorted as if it weren't possible.

"Ol' Tug was a natural. Water skiing was in his veins. He lived for it."

My thoughts went back to skiing with Grandpa Tug. How he had stood in the shallow water to help me put on my skis. That had been a much simpler time, one when shed doors and lookouts weren't falling from the sky. A time when letting his dog poop in your yard was the worst thing a neighbor would ever do.

"Anyway, in light of your recent loss, I'd like you and your family to attend our fiftieth annual Fourth of July Lawnmower Race as my personal guests," the President said handing Abby five tickets.

"Wow! You mean like sitting in a suite with all you can eat and drink and stuff?" Kyle gushed.

"No, I mean by sitting in the grandstands wearing these," Harley said unraveling a blue T-shirt that read 'Vote Harley'.

Abby wrinkled her nose at the shirt. I knew exactly what she was thinking. She wouldn't be caught painting the cottage in that shirt. Suddenly Wilbert Harley seemed less like a president and more like some lousy Santa Claus. Of course, the biggest difference was he didn't arrive behind a team of reindeer, was missing the beard and his gifts sucked.

After all who would want to go watch someone racing lawnmowers? I mean running up and down a lawn, back and forth, back and forth doesn't exactly sound like thrilling stuff. Well I guess Dad might because he was always so proud of our yard and the job he did mowing it, but then again he also seemed oddly proud of the fact he never stopped the toilet up, too.

The President continued, handing Kyle five T-shirts. "Anyway, I heard through the grapevine your parents might be looking to sell the cottage?"

Nobody responded. Somewhere a weed eater whirred loudly. Before I could say anything, Wilbert Harley began falling over himself with a skittish apology, "Not that I'm interested in buying it or anything. What happens to your family cottage is your business! It's just that…you know, part of my job as president is to keep on top of property matters up here." The man put one hand on his round belly and smiled. "That's the only reason I ask."

"Is it true there are thirty-five bathrooms in the White House?" Abby asked.

Wilbert Harley looked at my sister as if she had three eyes. "Why didn't you just buy Jimmy Longstockings' cottage?" I asked, my mouth once again failing to follow direct orders from my brain to stay closed.

A strange look spread over the man's face. He didn't offer an answer. Instead, his pudgy fingers took a moment to explore his generous belly. "Sooo-anyway, if you find out your parents are considering selling, why don't you have them give me a call? You know, I might be able to put them in touch with a buyer or something like that. It was really great to meet you kids. Now get out there and have a great Bass Lake day!"

Eric Walker Williams

We watched the President waddle down to Lake Road where he was met by Art Guilafante. The two stood shoulder to shoulder, talking in the shade of the coffee trees.

"Wow, we just met the President!" Abby gawked, staring across our deck toward the little round man. "He looks a lot taller on TV."

I glanced at my sister. It always amazed me how she was the oldest yet still needed an endless supply of things explained to her. I set my eyes back on the President and the Big A. Sunlight flitted through the coffee leaves cutting Art's face into a jigsaw pattern, making him look more evil.

"Did you see the President's face?" I asked.

"Yeah, great tan." Abby answered quickly.

"No, I mean when I asked about Jimmy's cottage? He got this real weird look on his face. It was like he knew something. Something he wanted to hide."

"Jack Nicholson had the same look in *A Few Good Men*."

"You realize Abby and I have never even heard of that movie, right?"

"He was hiding something. Nicholson I mean, not President Harley."

"How could someone claim to know all about properties up here and then not know Jimmy had sold his?" I offered.

"You know, I used to like coming up here." Kyle said, squinting at the duo down on Lake Road. "But now it's just getting too weird. It's starting to remind me of Bodega Bay."

"What bay?" Abby asked.

"Bodega Bay. You know from Hitchcock's movie *The Birds*? Really creepy," Kyle declared with wide eyes, "And we all know how that one ended."

A quiet moment hung before I finally turned to Kyle. "You realize neither one of us have any idea how that one ended, right?"

"Let's just say it wasn't good." He answered shortly.

"The movie?" Abby asked.

"No, the ending. The movie was amazing, the ending wasn't good. I mean it was a great ending as far as movie endings go, but bad things happened. Really, really, *really* bad things."

Harold Farcus had turned his bucket hat toward Lake Road. He was keeping one eye on the Big A and one on President Harley at the same time. It was clear from the strange way he was holding Larry closer to his chest that Harold thought something really, really bad was about to happen on the lake.

16

～～～～～～

Art Guilafante seized me with his large, thick hands. In one quick motion, he started spinning me around like a human helicopter. I was moving so fast the air being forced through my ears registered as a furious whir. Then, with a devilish grin on his big round face, Art dropped me into a coffin with a dull klunk. The sunlight slowly faded as he lowered the lid of the casket on me, sealing it with a shoosh. Whir, klunk, shoosh…whir, klunk, shoosh. I began pounding as hard as I could on the casket lid. The sounds only grew louder. Whir, klunk, shoosh. Whir, klunk, shoosh. I opened my mouth to scream but the only noise that would come out was a whir, a klunk and a shoosh.

I jerked up out of bed. The alarm clock read 3:25. Whir, klunk, shoosh…whir, klunk, shoosh. It had all been a dream but the noises were still there. My thoughts jumped to the Big A. Was it a chainsaw? Was he outside trying to cut our cottage in half?

All my parents wanted to talk about was 'bad luck'. How what we'd endured, all these so called accidents, were simply an amazing streak of really bad luck. I couldn't help but think, if this was bad luck, it was a 'Smash a mirror over your head while riding a black cat under a ladder on Friday the 13th' kind of bad luck.

There remained absolutely no doubt in my mind, Art Guilafante was a killer. When he was out watering his lawn I knew he was just loosening the soil so digging a shallow grave for my family would be all the more easy.

When I saw him jogging along Lake Road, I knew it was more than just exercise. Art was training for the day he'd have to outrun the police after it was discovered how he'd 'offed' three innocent children. Grandpa Tug always said fences make the best neighbors. After meeting Art Guilafante, I had decided I wouldn't feel safe at Bass Lake until our cottage was surrounded by the Great Wall of China.

Whir, klunk, shoosh. The sound kept coming in a steady rhythm. Something sent my feet to the floor. Maybe it was the fact falling asleep was proving difficult considering the collapse of the lookout still had me rattled. More likely it was the fact I needed to catch Art in the act, so everyone would stop thinking I'd lost my mind.

"Kyle," I whispered, nudging him in the shoulder.

"Keep the sand out of your weapons," he muttered, still asleep, "Keep those actions clear. I'll see you on the beach."

"Kyle!" I whispered louder, nudging harder. Whir, klunk, shoosh came the noise from outside. "Get up already, there's somebody outside!"

A quiet moment followed. I heard my brother roll over. Then he began muttering in a sleepy voice. "Every time you salute the Captain, you make him a target for the Germans!"

"Kyle! This is for real, get up already."

"What is it?" He whined.

"I think its Art. I think he's trying to saw our cottage in half!"

He rolled away from me, jerking the covers over his head. "Wait till morning. I'll go with you then."

"What about the *Curse of Bass Lake*? You might be able to get some really great night footage!"

"Too dark," he groaned through a yawn. "The aperture on my camera's all wrong for it."

The stairs squeaked under my feet. Our living room was black, but I navigated the darkness with ease because no furniture had been moved since my dad had taken his first steps. The backdoor squealed as I pushed it open. I eased my way onto the concrete pad behind the cottage.

The soft drumming of frogs in the night was broken up by another whir, klunk, shoosh. It was much louder now and was clearly coming from Weird Harold's back yard.

The air was brisk and the world seemed frozen under the light of a late moon. A cluster of horse weeds cast their shadows in front of me. Like arms and hands and fingers, they seemed to be reaching out for me, longing to drag me into Weird Harold's world. The one where up is down and being backward is normal and personal hygiene of any type is fiercely frowned upon.

I took a small step toward Harold's cottage and suddenly the world came alive as the wind rushed up and battered the trees. The sound roared like ocean waves crashing ashore. From down by the lake came the clanking of metal. The pontoon boats were moving on the waves. It was a restless noise, like horses shifting in their stables. And then the wind was gone, only to be replaced by the distant barking of an angry dog.

Whir, klunk, shoosh. The dog sent my mind racing. What if I wasn't the only one prowling around out here? I held my breath and listened. I could feel eyes on me as if somebody was watching, stalking me like a wolf in the shadows. I stopped to train my ears for the sounds of Art's heavy breathing or snarl of the alpha male, but could only hear the blood gushing through my veins. Whir, klunk, shoosh. Quick as it came, the noise was gone.

The world around me was dark and empty. Things I knew were there: the pile that had been Grandpa Tug's lookout, his shed, the old abandoned boat lift draped in ivy, had all vanished in the darkness.

Then it came again. Whir, klunk, shoosh. My feet inched toward Harold's backyard, each step less confident than the one before. The boards on Harold's fence were mismatched and heaved in one direction before twisting over on itself. In the darkness the fence looked like some massive prehistoric snake with a stegosaurus spine. Grandpa Tug may have said 'fences make the best neighbors', but I was pretty sure he hadn't been talking about this one. Too high to see over, I crept to the one place a single, ill-fated board had tumbled into a grave of ivy and prickle weeds. The board's untimely death provided a perfect space for spying on Weird Harold.

As I stuck my face to the opening, I was greeted with another whir, klunk, shoosh. It came bursting out with such vigor and force it nearly knocked me off my feet. Even amidst the darkness, the shadowy figure of Weird Harold Farcus could be seen. His face was black as night, but the outline of that bucket hat gave him away. Whir, klunk, shoosh.

Busy as a beaver, he was at the controls of a small digging machine. It spun with a loud whir. It klunked when he stopped it and shooshed as he emptied his bucket. The little digger swung back and forth violently, jolting Harold in his seat like a rodeo cowboy. Scoop after scoop, Harold's pile grew slowly. Scoop after scoop, the hole got deeper. Whir, klunk, shoosh.

Harold was working feverishly, as if reaching China by morning were a realistic goal of his, and the way he was working, you would believe it was entirely possible. That white bucket hat danced on his head as the digger spun around with robot-like precision, jerking him left, then right, then back again.

Harold was just being Harold. Grandpa Tug always said life was full of things you would never understand, and at that moment, no truer words had been spoken. Turning away, I hurried back to the cottage. For the rest of the night, Harold's whirs, klunks and shooshes echoed over the lake.

17

~~~~~~~

Boat rides are supposed to be relaxing. Well, I know the Titanic probably wasn't all that relaxing, but boat rides on Bass Lake are supposed to be. The hum of the engine, the gentle rocking of the hull. It's enough to put most twelve year olds to sleep, but at that moment, striking out across Bass Lake in Grandpa's Toy, relax was something I could not do. There were simply too many unanswered questions.

Questions or not, my dad was determined to get us on the water, so there we were, the boat slicing across the lake like a hot knife through butter. My dad was in control, his hands perched with pride on the large pearl white steering wheel. People slowed to watch the old wood boat cruise by. They gawked as if we'd been shot straight out of a time machine. Men pointed and women took pictures. Grandpa's Toy was truly something to see.

"So, how's *The Curse of Bass Lake* coming along Kyle?" Mom asked, her voice struggling against the droning of the engine.

"It's been slow," my brother admitted.

"Yeah, he's having trouble finding anything dangerous or suspenseful about the lake," I added quickly. "Because it's so boring up here. You know, nothing strange or bizarre ever happens."

"Careful, Kayla Marie," my dad started in, "There's an awful lot of boats out here to be out treading water by yourself. Could be dangerous."

I snorted loudly, "Yeah, I wouldn't know anything about dangerous things or almost dying, Dad."

"Hey, that's where they used to have the ski ramp Grandpa Tug went over when I was a kid," Dad explained, pointing at an empty spot on the water.

Kyle followed Dad's finger with his camera. "That's awesome, Dad. Do you know if there's ever been any ghost sightings there? Maybe some scary stories? A fatal skiing accident? Sinking boats?"

"Don't know anything about that, but speaking of skiing, anyone want to try?"

"And mess my hair up, Dad? No thanks!" Abby snarled.

"Maybe tomorrow," Kyle answered quickly. Of course, everyone in the family knew 'maybe tomorrow' was standard Kyle speak for 'I'm terrified and won't ever do it'.

"There's some really good water out here, buddy," Mom explained. "It would be a great time to try."

"Over there used to be an ice cream stand you could pull your boat right up to," Dad said nodding at the shore. A cluster of construction equipment now stood where 'Dooley's Ice Cream to Go' had once been.

My eyes wandered down the shore. Dogs were busy chasing Frisbees as people tossed footballs around or sat together in the sun, and the cottages, the beautiful, beautiful, triangle shaped cottages all lined up in a row ringing the lake. American flags fluttering off their porches.

The water rushed by as I laid my head back and closed my eyes. The warmth of the sun spilled over my face. The breeze was soft and heavy. All the chaos and weirdness I'd been through since we'd returned to the lake began to melt away, lost in the engine's hum.

For a moment, everything was perfect. The gentle rocking of the boat, the heat from the sun. Then I felt my body growing colder. A pool of water was crawling over my feet. Above the roar of the engine, I heard Dad explaining to my mom, "It's best to get her out and warm her up before you start pulling skiers."

"Dad!?" I shouted nervously. "Why's there water in the back of the boat?"

By the time he'd turned around, Kyle and I were sitting in water over our ankles. I can't repeat exactly what my father said at that point; but if ever a situation called for that combination of words, he'd found the right one.

"Do something!!" I screamed.

Dad jerked the wheel around turning a perfect dog bone while heading back toward the cottage. He slammed the throttle forward causing the engine to roar louder. The old boat rose from the water while gathering speed.

With water up to my knees, the cottage was still a good 300 yards away. That's when Grandpa's Toy began to slow down, as if someone on the far side of the lake had tied a rope to her stern and was tugging us backwards.

Kyle and I scrambled to the front as the water kept rising. With both hands clamped to the wheel, Dad rose to his feet. He was trying to see over the nose of the old boat, as the bow was busy climbing higher. Before anyone could speak, the roar of the engine died. The motor housing was completely underwater. With two hundred yards left to shore, the boat was half gone.

That's when Dad said it. Two words that will haunt me forever. Two words you *never* want to hear when you're riding on a boat.

"Everyone overboard!"

18
~~~~~~~

Nobody moved. My dad had given the command to abandon ship, but we all sat still, staring at him in disbelief. Grandpa's Toy was half in the water now. Could this really be happening *again?*

"Let's go! Jump out!!" Dad yelled, shooing us toward the water with his arms.

His tone forced us all to scramble off the boat. I leapt from the side, plunging deep into the cool lake. When I came up, Dad was standing on the nose of Grandpa's Toy, tossing kapok cushions down at us. Then, just as the chrome housing of the navigation lights slipped below the water, Dad stepped off at the last possible moment. The sight sent a chill up my spine. Grandpa's Toy was gone.

"What do we do now?" My mom asked clinging to her seat cushion, chin barely above the water.

Kyle was next to me, floating with one hand extended in the air, protecting his precious camera. "Someone will come get us," Dad answered. "There's too many boats out here. It's not like we were on the Titanic. This isn't the North Atlantic." Before Kyle could find a line from the movie *Ti-*

tanic to use, a high pitched whine filled the world around us. It sounded like three million bumble bees screaming into the same megaphone.

What happened next was straight out of a horror movie. Once again, just as I had survived another accident that should have ended my all too short life, the same man showed up just as he had so many times before.

It was the Big A, and this time he'd brought the whole family. The Guilafantes looked like a school of sharks, each on their own multi-colored wave runner, darting to and fro and circling around each other. Art was wearing a neoprene jacket and aviator sunglasses, as he corkscrewed in the water before jumping across his own wake. He landed in a nose-dive, sending a blast of water across his chest.

"Awesome!" Kyle chirped excitedly.

That's when he turned around and started riding straight for us. Well, straight for me. I closed my eyes. There was nothing I could do but brace for the inevitable. This was it.

If my life was supposed to be flashing before my eyes, it wasn't. All I saw was the nose of Art Guilafante's wave runner racing at me like a torpedo. Then, at the last possible moment just inches from my head, he turned suddenly and sent another tiny tsunami of water over me.

"What happened!?" He asked, killing his engine.

"Just having a little boat trouble, that's all, Art," my dad confessed. I noticed a slight twinge of frustration in his voice. Was he finally starting to see things the way I did?

This was more than boat trouble, and Art knew it. This was also more than dumb luck, and Art knew it. I was starting to lose track of all the times I'd almost died, only to have Art Guilafante show up.

"Don't worry. We'll get you guys out of here," Art promised. "Taryn, you get the two girls. Russ, grab Kyle, and Mom will pick up Kathy."

Taryn Guilafante looked down her skinny nose at me. Her hair was pulled back in a pony tail, and she wore dark sunglasses. She looked every bit as annoying and obnoxious as her father. She was dwarfed by her giant wave runner. The motor gurgled and growled as she struggled to turn it toward me.

"I didn't know the marina rented jet skis, Art," my dad said, pulling himself up on Art's machine.

"They don't. We just bought these this morning."

"You *bought* four of them?" Kyle gushed.

"How capitalistic of you," I sneered.

Art jumped at the chance to tell us all about his new toy, the 8700 something that had a load capacity of blah, blah, blah, blah, blah. It was all exhausting. He finished by patting the side of his machine as if it were a horse. "If it's all right with your dad, I'll let you ride one after lunch, Kyle."

Dad didn't answer. Instead he sat staring back at the water where Grandpa's Toy had been. His face was draped with shock, shock that she was really gone. Mom was too busy climbing onto Betsy Guilafante's wave runner to tell my brother no.

"Don't you think he's a bit young to be riding a jet ski?" I asked, assuming the role of parent since mine had temporarily abandoned their post. "I mean, I'd think if Kyle rode one, he would stand a good chance of being seriously hurt."

Without announcing it, I was subtly trying to get Art to come out into the open. To admit what he was doing to my family. I'd seen my share of cop shows and knew that sometimes even the slickest criminals can be tricked.

"Nonsense! Russ was riding them when he was five!"

"That sounds extremely safe," I fired back. "If he's lucky, maybe you'll get him some dynamite sticks or razor blades for Christmas this year."

"Zip it, Kay!" my dad snapped. Though he had taken a break from parenting to mourn the loss of Grandpa's Toy, my father's timing remained remarkably reliable as always.

"You guys are on some kind of bad luck streak, that's for sure!" Art said, steering his machine in a circle to aim it at our cottage. "Can't say as I've ever seen anything like it before in my life. It's almost like someone doesn't want you up here!"

For the first time since arriving at Bass Lake, Art Guilafante had finally said something I agreed with. We were finally on the same wavelength. Two minds, completely opposite, moving in the same direction for once. The only trouble was, in this case, the someone who didn't want us up here was him.

There comes a time every evening when the activity on Bass Lake settles down. Grandpa Tug called it the 'golden hour'. This is the time when the rays of the sun bathe everything with a tint of gold, as it fights an inevitable slide below the horizon. Boats are lifted from the water as children hustle around putting tubes and skis away. If timed right, one can sit on the shore and hear nothing but the rippling water. No whining jet skis or rumbling ski boats. During the golden hour, the lake catches its breath from a long day of busy activity.

Most families huddle inside their cottages for dinner when the golden hour comes. The lake is left for the kingfishers and the occasional blue heron. Grandpa Tug always said the herons had learned over the years that the fishing was best on Bass Lake when the families were busy eating too.

Grandpa always dragged me down to the water during the golden hour. We'd sit stone still on his bench. There was something magical about it. Just the two of us sitting on the pier, watching the lake returning to its normal state.

This was another reason the Big A didn't fit in at Bass Lake. His life was the complete opposite of the golden hour. He was loud, obnoxious, and never took time to relax. Art was outside cursing and waving a broom around in the air during the golden hour. Watching the man through our dining room window, he looked completely ridiculous.

As the rest of the lake was taking a breath and putting their feet up, Art was howling around trying to tear Bud and Ella's nest down. Little Bud flitted around the Big A's big head, trying his best to stop the man from destroying his life's work. Art's face was racked with rage as he slammed the broom against his cottage. With each blow, the earth seemed to shake beneath my feet. Art looked like a mad man. Then in one swift move the Big A swung and knocked Bud and Ella's nest to the ground where it shattered into dozens of pieces. Ella raced away as Art trained his broom on Bud. The little swallow dodged the swinging stick, bravely buzzing the man's face. "If you don't get out of here, I'm going to kill you!" Art exploded.

A chill ran up my spine. Art's voice was so loud and booming, but the dining room in our cottage was as quiet as the golden hour. We'd all heard the man scream, but nobody

Eric Walker Williams

spoke of it. I watched my dad chewing his hot dog. His brow furrowed. There was a glint in his eye that said maybe, just maybe, he was beginning to think the same thing about our neighbor.

After an unusually quiet dinner, everyone pitched in to clean up as Dad bagged the trash. Kyle, Abby, and I followed him out to the shed, keeping a free eye out for Tricky.

"Grab the trash can," Dad said, wrapping the neck of the garbage bag with duct tape. As Dad kept busy, I found myself glancing around nervously. I don't know what I was worried about more, finding Tricky waiting for our garbage, or the thought of Big Art Guilafante lurking in the shadows.

Kyle slid the can over to my dad as he dropped the bag inside. "Put the lid on," he ordered. "This will fix that good-for-nothing oversized rat." my dad bristled, tugging a concrete block up from the floor of the shed. He planted it on the lid of the trash can.

"You know, Dad, if you want to keep him out of the trash, why don't you just close the shed door?" Abby offered.

A quiet moment hung in the air as we all waited patiently for Abby to remember the fact that two days ago the shed door had collapsed. "Oh yeah," she groaned quietly, "Good idea... the block! There's no way that good-for-nothing, garbage-eating, make-up-wearing, ring-tailed- rat will get in there now!"

"He won't move that thing in a million years," Dad announced with pride, beaming at the concrete block. "I'll bet it weighs four times more than he does."

Upon returning to the cottage, Kyle and I dove into a game of Monopoly. Abby headed for the couch and buried her nose in a magazine. It wasn't long before we heard our mother's voice coming from the kitchen.

"Honey, I'm not sure, but I think I hear him in the shed again."

My dad came racing through the dining room. I dropped my thimble and tiny plastic house to follow him. From the back steps we heard Tricky's claws scraping across the lid of the trash can.

"What's wrong?" Dad asked, basking in his moment of victory. "Having trouble?"

When we entered the shed, Tricky sat up and cocked his head as though he might have an answer. My pulse quickened at the sight of the raccoon. He was bigger than I had thought. Apparently, a life-long steady diet of garbage had been very good to him.

"Having trouble with the lid?" Dad asked, his voice wrapped in sarcasm as he stepped closer. Tricky ran his little paw across his muzzle and blinked. Then in a flash, he shoved the block off the can. Before my dad could even flinch, the block had fallen onto his bare foot, crushing it into the hard concrete floor.

My dad doesn't cuss very often, but when he does, he gets his money's worth. He let a trail of expletives fly that would have sent Grandma Minnie scrambling for the bar soap. As he was cursing aloud, he started hopping around the garage on one foot as if he were riding a pogo stick. I covered my face in embarrassment.

Tricky hissed and snickered, before flipping the lid off to dive into the garbage. "Grab the bat Kyle!!" My father commanded through pain.

Kyle raced to the corner of the shed and grabbed a baseball bat. "Cream him!!" Dad shouted. "Hit the can! *Hit* it!"

Peeking through my fingers, I saw my brother taking aim. With one swift move, he drove the bat down toward the can. That's when Tricky quickly hopped out, upsetting the can. With the garbage can now on it's side, Kyle whiffed over it with his bat.

Of course, whiffing is part of baseball. It happens all the time. Nobody blinks at a whiff. Unless of course it comes in the ninth inning of the Cook County World Series with two outs and your team losing. However, this particular whiff hurt just as much, for when my brother whiffed over the can, the bat didn't stop until it had slammed into my dad's last good leg.

"OOOOOOOOWWWWWW!" Dad screamed, dropping to the floor.

Tricky sat up on his haunches for a moment and cackled out loud. I watched before lowering my head even further in shame as Tricky jollily bounded down the drive out of sight. Down by Lake Road, Harold's rangy figure could be seen lurking in the shadows. Somewhere beneath that bucket hat I just knew Weird Harold was fighting back a smile.

19

~~~~~~~

Summers at Bass Lake aren't complete without Jarts. A contest of skill, I never thought of Jarts as a deadly game until I saw Art Guilafante playing next door. Lobbing one Jart after another skyward, none of them landing anywhere close to the target ring lying harmlessly in the grass.

With all I'd been through, something as harmless as a game of Jarts became life and death. Suddenly, a Jart seemed like a weapon from the First World War. Armed with a steel tip and plastic wings, it is designed to rise and fall in a direct line, with the goal being to either hit the plastic ring, or impale your opponent. Cowering in my lawn chair with Jarts flying all around, I struggled with the first line of my apology: 'Dear Art, I am sorry all your efforts to kill us have failed.'

That seemed a bit strong. "What about this?" I asked Kyle before reading aloud, "Dear Art, thank you for almost killing my brother and I with your float plane. I am sorry for snooping in your shed. P.S. You are evil. Best Wishes, Kyle and Kayla."

Kyle was watching some of the video he'd shot on his camera. "I like it, but you know Mom and Dad won't go for it." he said, without looking up.

This was going to be harder than I thought. Hopefully I'd luck out and my parents would forget our punishment. Mom emerged from the cottage with a wicker basket in hand.

"Well I finally got all the weeds cleared out of Grandpa's garden," she announced. "Believe it or not, there's still some stuff growing in there."

I covered my note with my hand quickly as Mom stopped in front of me. "I picked some scallions and cleaned and cut them. I'm going to leave some in this basket for when you go over to make your apology to the Guilafantes. It will make a nice gift." She made busy rearranging the plants in her basket as she went on. "Your dad and I are going into town to get some groceries. No swimming until we get back. Abby has her cell phone to call us if anything else happens."

I was fully aware of the fact Abby had a cell phone, because I didn't. In fact, hearing Mom repeat it only made it seem all the more unfair.

"You want some popcorn?" Kyle asked, his eyes still locked on the video screen of his camera.

"Popcorn? How can you think of popcorn at a time like this?"

"Because if we're really going over there to let Art kill us, I'm at least going to have some popcorn first."

"That's really what you would want for your last meal?"

"Whoa!" Kyle yelled in a subtle roar, eyes locked on the camera screen. "Was that what I thought it was?"

"What is it?"

"Oh my gosh! Kay! You're not going to believe this!"

"What is it already?"

"Look at this," he said, leaning over to show me the camera. "I was taking this the other day. You know, the day the President came over? This was before he showed up, when you and I were in the front yard playing cornhole?"

The camera wobbled in Kyle's nervous hands. There was a shot of me throwing a cornhole bag. "So what? I know I'm terrible at cornhole--"

"—No, look behind you."

Kyle ran the video back, so I could see it again. This time I noticed a large dark figure moving across Lake Road behind me. "Is that Art?" I asked.

"You know anyone else that big? That's not all, check out what's in his hand."

"I don't see anything."

Kyle ran the video back further and sure enough, Art's hand was definitely carrying something in it.

"This was when Mom and Dad left for their walk. Remember? They asked the Guilafantes to go with them?"

The video was blurry at best. Art's figure appeared only as a grainy shadow. His arm was extended away from the camera, but his hand was definitely carrying something. "It almost looks like a gun, but why would Art be carrying a gun toward the lake?"

"It is a gun," Kyle answered quickly. "A screw gun, just like the one we found on the floor of Art's shed the other day."

"You mean...the one with the..."

"Drill bit," Kyle and I said in unison.

"Can you blow it up?" I asked.

"Not without my laptop. I left that at home."

"Why would Art be taking a screw gun down to the water?"

My eyes floated over to Art. He was lobbing Jarts high in the sky, laughing with his kids. Even when he wasn't trying to look evil, somehow he could still pull it off. His big head began to swing my direction, so I shifted my stare down to the lake. The Indian grass swirled along shore, and just beyond stood Grandpa's boat lift. A skeleton now, it looked naked without Grandpa's Toy sitting on it.

"Grandpa's Toy!" I shrieked, catching myself at the last moment so Art wouldn't hear. "Grandpa's Toy!" I whispered, "The drill bit you stepped on! It wasn't just any old drill bit! That drill had a paddle bit on it!"

"A what bit?" Kyle repeated.

"A paddle bit!"

"And you know what a paddle bit is because?"

"They're for boring holes in wood! Grandpa used them when we built the houses for the woodies!"

"Kayla, are you sure?"

"Kyle, I know a paddle bit when I see one. I just didn't think twice about it until…"

"Until Grandpa's Toy sank?"

My eyes fell on our neighbor. The Big A's enormous, sasquatch-like feet were standing naked in the grass. His golden aviators shining brightly in the sun. His son Russell looked pretty good, because every Jart he tossed wound up spiking in the ground pretty close to the plastic ring.

Art was another story. His throws were all over the place. One even struck the side of their cottage, causing Bud and Ella to dart away quickly. The Jart's metal spike gashed the cedar siding. "Kyle…tell me this isn't real."

"No. It's real all right, its right here. We have video evidence now, Kay."

"I don't know. It's really grainy. I mean, it's like a Sasquatch video. You can't really make anything out."

"Well, I can tell it's a really tall dude carrying what looks like a gun toward the water where we always kept Grandpa's Toy on the lift."

My eyes returned to the Jart game. Every toss made my heart skip. The fear Art might send a misguided Jart my way took over my body. Of course calling the Jart misguided would be in itself misguided, because Art would be most definitely guiding his Jart toward me on purpose.

That's when it hit me. Something falling from the sky. Was it a Jart? I looked down expecting to find myself covered in blood, but there was none. Surely a Jart would have pierced my heart or cracked my skull open.

Whatever this was had bounced off my head and was now resting in the grass beside me.

It was a piece of paper, crumpled into a small ball. My heart began thundering.

Where had it come from? I looked over at the Guilafantes. Art was giving Russell a noogie as his wife and daughter were busy laughing hysterically. On the other side, Haorld's yard was empty. Well, save the concrete statue of Mary, sprawling clusters of tomato plants, and jungle of horseweeds, but Harold was nowhere to be seen.

Looking around cautiously, I reached down and unraveled the wad of paper. Art's voice boomed over a Jart throw as I read the note:

Goat Drop: 11:30

Eric Walker Williams

"What do you think it means?" Kyle asked after we'd relocated to the safety of the kitchen.

"I think someone wants to meet us at the goat drop today," I answered quickly, hoping someone would volunteer to go.

"What do you mean, us?" Kyle asked.

"It's a pronoun," I explained. "It implies that you and I will both be going to the goat drop."

"Yeah, but they threw the note at you, not us," Kyle said.

"We're twins, genius. That means we stick together."

"Let's go tomorrow," Kyle suggested.

"The note says today at 11:30."

"I'm on record as saying this is a bad idea," Abby said, completely avoiding my brother's weak attempt at dodging the trip.

"I'm with Abby. This sounds like a trap," Kyle started in. "Stuff like this is always a trap in the movies. You wind up with crashing cars and buildings falling down and massive explosions and the main character fighting some goon on the ledge of a really tall building overlooking all the car crashes, falling buildings, and explosions."

Abby and I stopped and gave our brother the strange look he deserved before continuing. "How could it be a trap?" I asked.

"What if Art wrote it?" Kyle suggested. His voice dropped low while finishing, "Maybe he wants to make you an offer you can't refuse. You know, like Don Corleone?"

"Don Corleone?"

"The point is, what if Art wants us to show up at the goat drop so he can grab us and bury us under one of his condos?"

My mind went back to being in Art's shed and fumbling for the light. The darkness had been so thick we couldn't make anything out. But now, just like that moment I'd found the light switch, Kyle's idea helped me see everything clearly. How could I have missed the obvious? I hadn't even considered the note might be from the Big A. I wasn't so sure about going anymore. I'd never considered a goat drop to be dangerous, but at that moment it had become clear this would be no ordinary goat drop.

Art Guilafante was even big when he slept. His snore was louder than a freight train. I was kneeling behind a bush between our cottages, watching him swinging in his hammock. Above him, Bud and Ella were busy rebuilding what was left of their nest. Bud placing the daubs of mud with care as Ella kept a nervous eye on Art.

After forming the bowl of the nest, Bud went back to the shore where he'd stumbled across some goose feathers. He carefully lined their little home using these and some short grasses. The breeze lifted one stray feather into the air. Ella watched it waft down toward Art before landing on his nose. The man let out a sneeze so explosive it seemed to rattle the windows of his cottage.

Ella fidgeted on her limb, keeping a wary eye on Art. Though he wrestled around in his hammock, he was soon soundly snoring again. Bud hopped on the rim of the nest and gave the all clear as Ella quickly flitted over to their new home.

I glanced at my watch. It was almost 11:00. Art was in a bellowing slumber in the shade. He wasn't going anywhere.

Eric Walker Williams

It would take me a half an hour to ride to the other side of the lake. There was no time to waste if I was going to make the Goat Drop in time.

20
~~~~~~~

"May the force be with you, Kay."
I stood with one foot in the door and one out. Was this the way my brother was going to send me off to the goat drop? Sitting on the couch, as if the seat of his shorts were stitched to the cushion?

"I can't believe you're making me do this alone."

"Strong am I with the force, but not that strong," Kyle responded quickly.

"This is a really bad time for your stupid, dumb movie quotes. Art Guilafante could be luring your twin sister into a trap, and you can't even get off the couch?"

"Just means more candy for me on Halloween, more presents at Christmas, more popcorn on movie night. The more I think about it, it's actually a pretty sweet deal. Besides, I already went with you to make the apology. I've risked my life enough today."

Figuring we would take our chances with Betsy Guilafante instead of Art, Kyle and I made our apology while the Big A was asleep in the hammock. I guess it went okay. Betsy had really liked the basket of scallions.

"Art just loves onions!" she gushed. "I'm going to make you two a big plate of cookies for this. Thank you so much!"

Of course, we didn't tell her that, as long as they were made by someone named Guilafante, there wasn't a cookie big enough, good enough or chocolate-y enough for us to eat…ever!

I guess the thought was somewhat nice, but my focus was on the goat drop now. My brother wasn't budging. I knew he could be hard headed. After all he was my twin, but before I had the chance to just give up and leave, Abby entered the room, leafing through a magazine. I knew I couldn't trick Kyle into going, but my older sister…

"Hey, Abby, so I'm going to the Goat Drop for my secret meeting. You know, the one where our neighbor might be waiting to squash me like a bug under his shoe? Anyway, don't you think it's a good idea for Kyle to come along with me? You know, that whole strength in numbers thing?"

My question didn't faze Abby. Her eyes remained locked on the pictures in her precious magazine.

"Of course you realize, there's a chance we might not come back at all. Just think Abby, more presents for you at Christmas, more popcorn on movie night? More money for Mom and Dad to spend on *just* you?"

Abby froze in her tracks. Like a robot, her head tilted up before rolling over to Kyle who was still planted firmly on the sofa.

"Get up and go with Kayla, dorkface," she commanded.

"I'm not going anywhere, and you can't make me," Kyle barked back.

"Get up or I'm telling Mom and Dad what really happened to Mom's ceramic baby Jesus."

The ceramic baby Jesus? Well played, Abby, well played. "You wouldn't dare…" Kyle growled.

"Don't tempt me, bro."

Soon enough, Kyle and I were on our bikes headed down Lake Road.

Located at the east end of the lake, the town of Bass Lake wasn't much more than a courthouse surrounded by a square that included a couple restaurants, an antique store, and a laundromat.

Still, small or not, I had no idea where to start. I didn't even know what I was looking for. Kyle was convinced we'd find a man in a trench coat, sunglasses, and fedora waiting for us. "He's been a part of every secret meeting in every spy movie ever made," Kyle explained. "He'll hand you a brief-case with a note in it or a hot dog vendor will slip you a bun with a message scribbled on it in invisible ink."

We ditched our bikes in the alley between the Silver Dollar Laundromat and Mr. Happy Burger's diner. A mob of people had gathered on the square in the shadow of the courthouse dome. The goat drop was one of the most popular events of the Bass Lake Festival. It was also the closest thing the Lake had to Groundhog Day. Dodging bodies and ducking elbows, we made our way to the front row. A square had been roped off in front of the court house.

The square was divided into smaller squares, each with a number scribbled inside it using sidewalk chalk. At the edge of the rope stood three farmers in overalls, each tethered to a goat. A few official looking people with clipboards were busy petting the animals. The goat drop had attracted quite a crowd. There were old ladies and little kids. A Boy Scout was standing at attention as if he were carved from wood or had been told not to move if he wanted to earn his goat drop badge.

"Hey, look. There's the President again," Kyle said, pointing across the square.

His round little face was beaming in the sun while he kept busy shaking hands with the crowd. The President winked at someone while stroking his handlebar mustache. He stopped to kiss a baby. Hoisting the child in the air, the baby immediately began screaming as if President Harley were planning to eat it like a Happy Burger.

Nobody seemed to be looking for Kyle and me. All eyes were trained on the President and the square in the street and the three goats. They were the stars of this show after all. In the crowd, old men debated strategies, pointing busy fingers at the grid of numbers.

My watch read 11:34. If I wasn't home by 1:00, Abby was supposed to make up some reason for Mom and Dad to bring her to town. I wasn't sure which had me more rattled, Kyle's theory that the note was from Art or the fact my back-up plan hinged on my older sister.

The people clustered around me appeared normal sized. If Art were nearby, there was no way he could possibly blend in here. My eyes inspected every tall person I could find. A man with a straw hat, another dressed in a muscle T-shirt and Bermuda shorts. Though the Big A didn't seem like the straw hat type, I'd seen enough detective shows to know the best criminals always had a world class disguise.

"You see anything?" I asked.

"Only some giant, ten-foot-tall freak-bug," Kyle answered, pointing over my shoulder. I turned to find a black head with long antennae picking its way through the crowd.

Kyle was zeroing in on it with his camera. "This is going to be just what *The Curse of Bass Lake* needs! Can't you picture it? Giant ant t-shirts and coffee mugs. Giant ant toys at fast food restaurants. We've hit a gold mine, Kay. A gold mine!'

Trust me when I say it's a strange sight to behold an ant walking on two legs. Its long antennae flopped wildly in the air as the ant went about tapping kids on the shoulder. One after another, the children spun around only to immediately scream in horror upon finding a ten-foot-tall insect asking for a hug. Could this be Art?

My mind became flooded with thoughts of this creature coming after me, chasing me with a Jart or crawling out from under my bed. A clown walking around on stilts strolled past. While it seemed like the perfect metaphor for Art, I was thankful to see the clown was actually a woman.

"You don't want any numbers close to the corner or along the edges," a gravelly voice explained from behind me.

I turned around and found something familiar close by. Like an old friend I hadn't seen in years, there was the white bucket hat of Weird Harold Farcus.

Eric Walker Williams

21

~~~~~~~

Harold was standing uncomfortably close, keeping his face hidden behind a plume of cotton candy. "It's the crowd. They make the goats nervous so they drift toward the middle."

"Whoa," Kyle gasped. "It's weir-er, uh, strange, uh, hey there, Harold."

Harold nodded at the square as if eye contact made him uncomfortable. "Was it you? Did you throw the note over the fence?" I asked.

Harold paused to nibble at his cotton candy. His teeth, stained the color of apple cider, gnawed at the crystallized sugar like an angry beaver taking to a sapling. He glanced around nervously before swallowing a wad. "Noah's boat was made of wood."

Harold hadn't answered my question, which wasn't a total surprise.

"What do you mean? You wanted me to come all the way over here to tell me that?"

A small gleam filled Harold's eye. His lips seemed to curl into what I thought was a faint smile. "Means they've been makin' wood boats for an awful long time 'cause they don't sink...'less someone puts a hole in 'em first."

"So-what are you saying?" Kyle asked.

"Marina had checked the motor out the day before... couldn't be internal."

"We think Art did it, and we have video evidence!" Kyle burst.

My head was swimming. I heard a bell ring. The first goat was entering the square. Just as Harold had predicted, it ran for the center, avoiding the edges and corners. The crowd grew louder every time the little goat hovered over a new square.

"Thirty seven!" someone shouted.

My eyes flashed to Weird Harold. He was wrestling with a deep fried Twinkie on a stick. I didn't have time to figure out this sudden change. I chalked it up to another in a long list of explanations for how Weird Harold had come by his nickname.

Still the look in his strange eyes was clear. We were thinking the same thing about Big Art Guilafante. At that moment, so many things were racing through my mind, and none of them dealt with deep fried Twinkies.

"What did you find in Art's shed the other day?" Harold asked.

"A drill bit and some magazines addressed to Jimmy. We thought it was strange that if Jimmy moved to Florida, why didn't he forward his mail?"

"Makes sense to me," Harold mumbled, loose chunks of deep fried Twinkie spilling from his mouth. "Jimmy left in an awful hurry. So much so, I never saw a moving truck."

My throat went dry. If there was anyone on the lake that would have seen Jimmy moving out, it was Harold, and if Harold never saw a moving truck, that could mean only one thing. Jimmy didn't move any of his stuff to Florida.

On one hand, it was somewhat satisfying to know an adult actually believed us. On the other hand, that adult *was* Weird Harold. Even I knew the best legal team in the world would look foolish if their star witness was a person who liked to do his yardwork with heavy machinery at 3:30 in the morning.

"I've been up here a long time, kid," Harold continued, speaking through a haze of gnats hovering around his Twinkie on a stick. "Never seen anything like this summer...I told you this place could be dangerous." A wicked grin spread over his face as he seemed to be unbothered by the crowd of insects fighting to get inside his mouth.

In the shadow of his bucket hat, Harold's skin was wrinkled and chafed ash white. The craggy lines on his face were dark, as if filled with dirt. Patches of silver stubble poked through in random places along his jawbone, making it look like he had clusters of steel wool glued to his face. A stray swarm of gnats had moved from the Twinkie to Harold's ear, ducking in and out, savoring clumps of wax as if they were honey.

I wanted to ask Harold if he thought we were right. I wanted to ask him why Art would be doing all this, and why Harold was digging in his backyard at 3:30 in the morning. My lips pursed to ask, but in true Weird Harold fashion, he took the conversation in an entirely new direction. "Saw President Harley stopped by the other day. What was that ol' pot belly after?"

President Harley? The name sounded so official. There was only one man who deserved to be called 'the President' and he didn't live on a tiny lake in the Midwest. The real president had real responsibilities. Things that were far more important than watching lawnmower races and judging competitive eating contests.

"Just to introduce himself, I guess." I answered.

"He invited us to the lawnmower race, but our parents said we were too busy to go," Kyle added.

"Lawnmower race huh? Well, guess it's best you turned down that invitation," Harold explained, forcing down one final glob of deep fried Twinkie. A cloud of gnats swirled around his lips, fueled by the hope a loose crumb might come tumbling out.

"Why's that?" I asked.

"Grandstands collapsed. Bunch of people had to go to the hospital," Harold explained.

I almost fell over in the street. The grandstands? Collapsed? What were the chances? Thoughts of collapsing grandstands set off a string of dominoes twisting through my brain. I saw the President's strange wink, his card. The way he'd asked if we were selling our cottage.

"Twenty nine!!! Come on!! Twenty nine already, you stupid goat!" someone screamed.

"I guess that explains a lot then don't it?" Harold said somewhat satisfied.

Suddenly I was tangled up and lost somewhere deep inside Harold's logic. "Explains what exactly?" I prodded.

"Explains what Larry and I heard them two money grabbers sayin' down on Lake Road."

My eyes swelled as Weird Harold continued, "Slappin' each other on the back like long lost brothers. Ol' Art was telling the President that everything has a price tag."

"You think they were talking about our cottage?"

"Ol' Art, he's a lot like Larry," Harold explained, pausing to point his empty Twinkie stick at me. "When the snow flies, Larry likes to wear a hat on the count his ears don't have any fur. He knows he needs to keep 'em warm, otherwise they get frostbit."

I hung on for a moment waiting for Harold to bring his story back to Art. Instead, he went back to work cleaning the last bits of fried Twinkie from his stick, teeth chittering with machine-like precision.

"But what does that have to do with Art?" Kyle finally asked.

"Point is, they're both smart, boy."

While I appreciated Harold trying to explain himself, once again he was proving himself backward as the day is long. "But there's only one way to know for sure," the man continued, his mouth opening into a wide, jack-o-lantern-like smile. The condition of his cider colored teeth, now covered with an oozing slime dotted with chunks of Twinkie, made me shudder.

Again he was slow to finish his thought. "And that would be?" I nudged.

"Somebody needs to get into that cottage and get a good look at those blueprints of his."

"Blueprints? Art has blueprints?" Kyle wondered aloud.

"The blueprints!" I erupted. "Do you think that's what he had in that tube? The one he pulled from the cargo bin in his plane?"

"I reckon they were blueprints or a pool cue, and Art don't strike me as the pool shark type."

"Are you sure they're blueprints?"

"They might be maps. Maybe there's treasure buried under the lake!" Kyle swooned with wide eyes.

"Hard tellin', but if you really want to know what's goin' on up here, what kind of plans that city feller has for the lake, you're gonna to have to find your way into that cottage of his and get your eyes on those prints, sweetheart."

"But Mom and Dad won't want us going over there," Kyle warned. "Not with everything we've already said about the Big A."

"We're done telling Mom and Dad about this," I said. "They don't believe us, so we're going to solve this thing without them."

"But the footage? On the camera? Don't you want to—"

"No," I interrupted. "We're not showing them."

The crowd suddenly exploded. I glanced at the square and found fresh goat droppings lying on number twenty-one. "There's a winner!" one of the clipboard people shouted through a megaphone. "Twenty-one, twenty-one, redeem your ticket for a cash prize at the booth outside the courthouse."

"You mean all these people were waiting for some dumb goat to poop in some stupid square on the street?" Kyle asked Harold.

When we turned to welcome his explanation, Harold had vanished into the crowd. I looked for a bucket hat bobbing and weaving its way upstream, but found nothing.

"I just can't believe this many people were standing around waiting for a goat to poop in the street," Kyle repeated, gawking at the crowd, "and I didn't even catch it on film!"

In true Harold style, the man had left at a weird time. My heart said he had ticket number twenty-one and went to collect his money, but my head told me Harold had left so quickly, because well, he was just plain weird.

"It says here the grandstands at the old racing grounds were built in the 1890's," Kyle said, unfolding Dad's copy of the *Bass Lake Anchor*. He laid it out on the table with our sister sitting nearby Indian-style, filing her nails. "That makes them over 100 years old. This says they were the fourth largest set of wooden grandstands in the state."

"Well, they were bound to fall sometime," Abby pointed out.

"Come on, Ab. Something has to explain all this. These are more than just accidents! What about the drill? Kyle and I found a drill in Art's shed."

"You mean Art's shed? The one that's probably full of Jimmy's stuff?" Abby asked.

"Okay. Still, it was a drill and it had a wood boring bit in it. The same kind you would need if you were going to drill a hole through the hull of a boat."

"I'm no lawyer, but I'm fairly certain none of this is going to hold up in court, Kay. Nobody saw a hole in the hull. Nobody saw Art using that drill. Nobody saw him near Grandpa's Toy either."

"Says here twenty-four people went to the hospital with minor cuts and bruises," Kyle added.

"The President invited us to the race, Abby. Remember?"

"Doesn't mean he knew the bleachers were going to collapse. Besides, if he knew they were going to fall, why would he go to the race and sit in them? He could have been hurt too."

"He wasn't in the grandstands when they fell," Kyle answered, reading aloud from the paper. "President Harley was down on the infield, busy awarding the ribbon and gallon jug of goat's milk to the winner when the grandstand collapse occurred."

Silence fell over the table as Abby's file stopped saw-ing long enough for her eyes to focus on the paper instead. From down on Lake Road came the sound of a moped whizzing by. There was a brief moment where I thought we had my sister. For one fleeting instant the Queen of Hor-monestan didn't care about her own health or beauty. There was a suspicious look in her eye that said she still needed a moment to finish adding this all up. I thought we had an ally, a new partner, someone to bounce ideas off of and count on to foil Art's plans to scare us off the lake. Then, just as I was ready to welcome her aboard the bandwagon to capture Art Guilafante red-handed, the Queen made her opinion known.

"It's all hogwash," she declared, shifting her focus back to her fingernails.

That night after dinner I followed my dad and Kyle out to the shed to put the trash away. Dad was fighting a pretty serious limp from the last run-in with Tricky. He'd been complaining pretty much nonstop about the pain, and though she was only a nurse and not a doctor, Mom had prescribed him with some pretty strong over the counter medications.

Kyle stuffed the bag into the can before jamming the lid in place. Dad put a finger to his lips as we tiptoed to the back of the shed like Army Rangers. We took our bat-tle stations in a row of lawn chairs arranged along the back wall. Kyle sat empty handed, eyes peeled for Tricky. Dad had

Grandpa Tug's Arnold Palmer Series seven iron in hand, and this time I was entrusted with the bat.

The inside of the shed was completely black. A blood red moon was sneaking up behind the far side of the lake as we sat in a vacuum of silence. Dad hoped to catch Tricky up to no good, but I wasn't sure what we'd find first, Tricky out for another midnight gourmet meal of trash ala trash, or Art Guilafante sneaking over to sabotage another part of our cottage. The eerie tremolo of a loon rang out. Buried somewhere in the blackness, the cackling sound crept up my spine and set my hairs on end.

The first hour passed quickly. In the growing moonlight, we sat watching shadows creep across the drive. A belly full of spaghetti was tugging at my eyelids, but soon enough a long yawn from Kyle snapped me back to attention. The glowing red taillights of a car down on Lake Road crawled by. Still no sign of Tricky.

The shed was pitch black, yet I could feel eyes all around me as if someone were watching us. The more I thought about it, the more convinced I became the Big A was in the shed. If not in the shed, then lurking just outside it; hacksaw in hand. He was ready to saw our cottage in half or send a Kentucky coffee tree crashing through my bedroom window. Then came a strange sound outside. The crash of metal falling to the ground. It had to be Art. That clumsy ox must had tripped over something on the way to our cottage.

My hands gripped the bat tighter. I imagined shattering Art's kneecap. If I had my way I'd beat that Goliath all the way back to Chicago. Big Art Guilafante had picked the wrong lake to destroy.

I turned an ear to the crashing sound. The sizzle of cicadas fired up, drowning everything out. Goosebumps crawled up my arms when the cicadas stopped in unison, as if they feared Art Guilafante too. I wouldn't have admitted it to Kyle, but at that moment, I was scared.

"Maybe he's taken a night off," Kyle finally whispered.

We waited for a response, but instead of Dad's voice, the soft sound of snoring was all we heard. In the long shadows of the shed, Dad's head was cocked to one side resting on his shoulder. He was out cold.

Once again, my head fell in shame. There was no need to speak. Kyle and I got up and returned to the cottage together, leaving our father asleep in the chair, golf club in hand, eyes shut and mouth wide open.

22
~~~~~~~

The drum major wore a high plumed hat with a crest of gold. His patent leather boots slammed on the ground in perfect time. A sparkling baton spun wildly in his hands, as he kept his eyes pointed skyward.

The sun beat down on the band as the drum corps thundered down Lake Road. Red-faced teenagers with puffy cheeks struggled through the heat. July at the lake can be brutal. Most days the heat is so sticky and thick, it just hangs on you like a heavy winter coat.

The bright red flags of the color guard were next, spiraling through the air. A spirited tune hung over the lake as the Bass Lake High School Marching Band high-stepped past.

"I'd like to be in the color guard someday," Taryn Guilafante told me, her eyes following the flags.

"I'd like to be the drum major," I admitted without shame.

The Bass Lake Festival Parade was touted as the longest parade in the world. It started near the heron rookeries just outside of downtown. Those in the parade then had to march away from downtown for the seven miles it took to go around the lake. The big finish came when the parade passed through downtown Bass Lake.

While everyone was busy sitting along the road waiting for the parade, I spied Weird Harold in his yard carrying Larry around in one arm like a newborn child. He was busy straightening his Keep Out signs again. Every once in a while I caught a sideways glance cast at us from under that bucket hat.

The Shriners came next, riding their miniature go-carts. Racing in figure eights, the tassels of their funny fez hats trailed in the breeze. Kyle and Russ were watching the little go carts sputter around, nearly colliding with each other time and again.

"Whoa! Look at him!!" Kyle shrieked as one of the cars went up on two wheels, nearly capsizing into the pavement. He planted his camera against his eye and began tracing the movements of the cars.

The California County rescue equipment was next, sirens wailing and horns blaring. It was an old 1950's model fire truck, bright red with gold lettering on the door. Children sitting on folded fire hoses were tossing handfuls of candy down. So much candy was falling from the sky, the truck appeared to be an erupting volcano of molten hot sugar.

"Dude! Check out those crazy old bikes!" Russell Guilafante said as a group of antique cyclists made their way down the road toward us. The Huff and Puffers International Bicycle Touring Club pedaled by on their big wheels. Spinning along atop eight foot tall tires, they were a lopsided sight to behold.

"How do they get on those things?" I asked Taryn, wrinkling my nose in disbelief.

Next came an all-white van with a phone number painted down the side. It seemed harmless enough, until my

Eric Walker Williams

eyes fell on the driver's seat where I found the same costumed insect we'd seen at the goat drop. My heart skipped a beat. More disturbing still was the giant, ten foot tall termite riding atop the van. It wore an evil face with long pointy fangs and bug eyes the size of basketballs.

"What do you get a ten foot tall termite for Christmas?" my mom asked.

"I don't know, Mom, what do you get a ten foot tall termite for Christmas?" Kyle answered, playing along.

"Anything he wants!"

The rumbling thunder of an old muscle car chased the van down Lake Road. It was Wilbert Harley, and he looked quite presidential riding atop his 1964 Camaro. A hand painted sign taped to the door read: "Wilbert Harley-President of Bass Lake-Democrat".

"Bass Lake has a president?" Taryn asked as the car rumbled by.

'Operation Cowbird' had come to me that morning while watching Bud and Ella. They were on a new nest they'd built on the side of Art's cottage. Bud looked so proud. His little chest was puffed out as he went about showing Ella all the hard work he'd put into rebuilding their new home.

But as the couple were busy celebrating, someone was busy spying from nearby. A female brown headed cowbird. From a branch overhead, she was eyeing the swallow's new home. She thought it looked perfect too. That's when, as if Grandpa Tug himself were whispering in my ear, the single greatest idea ever came to me.

"Cowbirds are notorious for laying their eggs in another bird's nest and leaving them for someone else to raise," I explained to Kyle.

Of course he didn't really understand birds, so he had a befuddled look on his face. The same one a cow might have if you were asking it to lay eggs or trying to teach it geometry. "All we have to do is be nice to the Guilafantes for a day. They'll probably ask us to stay the night, and then, once we're inside the Big A's house and everyone's asleep, we can get a look at the blueprints Harold was talking about!"

So it was decided, we would use the parade to win the Guilafantes over. It would be easy. I even came up with a simple set of rules to make sure Kyle didn't screw the whole thing up like he had that day in Art's shed. I called them the Top Five Rules for Winning the Guilafante Kids Over:

1. Give them all your parade candy
2. Laugh at their jokes
3. Give them all your parade candy
4. Agree with whatever they say (it doesn't matter if it flies in the face of everything you've ever been taught or stood for as a person before in your life, just smile and agree)
5. Give them all your parade candy

So it was as Kyle and I were sharing seats next to Russ and Taryn Guilafante, the parade was rolling by in all its glory.

"Where's Art?" my mom asked Betsy Guilafante.

"You know, it's the strangest thing. We were getting ready to come out here, and he just laid down on the couch. He told Taryn his stomach was cramping up. He could probably use some sleep. He's been working so hard trying to get everything done. You know, the condos and spa and the parking lot. And I swear, that blasted golf course might be the end of him! They just can't figure out the best way to get that swamp drained. I do want to thank you for the scallions though. He had some with his salad for lunch."

"Well, I hope he's all right. It's just so awful to turn up sick like that in the middle of the summer."

Yeah it was awful all right. After all, I had replaced the scallions in Mom's basket with the rootstocks from a blue flag iris plant I found growing behind the shed. Grandpa always said animals stayed away from the iris because of the nasty stomach aches they caused. And, after hearing Betsy Guilafante complaining about finding a way to get the swamp drained, I wanted to suggest she try the scallions too.

"Where's Walt, Kathy?" Betsy asked.

"I'm not sure. When I got up this morning, he was gone. Maybe he ran in to town to get something."

A plastic elephant two stories high rolled by on a float. "But your car is still here," Betsy observed, pointing toward our cottage.

"Kyle? Where's your father?" Mom asked. "I thought he fell asleep on the couch again, but he wasn't there this morning and I haven't seen him all day."

Before Kyle could answer, I suddenly remembered Dad falling asleep in the shed. I grabbed Taryn's arm and led the way across Lake Road. We darted between the Bass Lake Festival Queen who was riding the lake's unofficial mascot, a donkey named Lucky, and the poor man chosen to carry a bucket and shovel behind Lucky.

When we arrived in the shed, the trash can was knocked over. Garbage was strewn everywhere. I began working my way to the back, sure to keep an eye open for any booby-traps the Big A may have left behind, and that's when we found him.

There in the back of the garage, still manning his post, and sound asleep, sat my father. It also appeared Tricky had shown up after all, for garbage was everywhere.

"What happened in here?" Taryn asked, covering her nose to filter the stench of rotting food.

The trash wasn't just scattered around my dad's chair. It was scattered *on* his chair as well. In fact, it was scattered all over him too. He was festooned with various food items. Bread crumbs dotted his pant legs. Banana peels straddled each arm and an empty potato chip bag sat on his head, looking more like a dunce cap.

Perhaps worst of all, we found Tricky's little paw prints all over his face. Bright, lipstick red tracks. The remnants of Mom's famous cherry pie.

"Does your dad always sleep in garbage?" Taryn asked.

"Not always," I admitted softly.

"That's pretty messed up."

"Yeah, he's pretty messed up all right," I sighed.

Before Taryn could respond, something stirred Dad from his slumber. His heavy eyes glanced over the garbage surrounding him. His head began shaking, slowly at first, and then more violently. Before I could think of anything to say, the vein on the side of Dad's head flashed from 'I'm sleeping' to 'Nuclear meltdown'. Taryn Guilafante's face wrenched up as my father's face burned into three shades of red before he finally erupted, "One of these days...I'm going to waterski on that lake wearing a coonskin cap!"

Once again my head fell in shame, and shame shared with the new neighbor girl I needed to impress was the absolute worst kind.

Eric Walker Williams

Later Taryn and I rode our bikes around the lake. We rode past cottage after cottage filled with families enjoying the sun. We rode out to where Lake Road takes the long bend around to the far side of the lake. I was relieved that there had been no accidents for me to survive during the parade. Still, convincing Taryn to ride around the lake had been a tough sell. She wanted to head straight for town to get ice cream. She'd also whispered something about looking for boys, but what I really wanted her to see was the swamp. Maybe if she saw everything her dad was going to ruin, I could convince her to stop him.

When the road curved back toward the water, the silver maples slowly emerged, their leaves shimmering in the hot midday sun. They rose above us like a row of medieval knights clad in armor, the swamp their castle. We welcomed their cool shadows while pedaling past.

"Did I tell you my dad's taking us to Vegas?" Taryn asked. The twinge of excitement in her voice told me she was 100% Guilafante. "Have you ever been?"

"No," I answered shortly.

"Vegas is amazing. There are like a bazillion lights and cool hotels shaped like pyramids. Our room is going to have two hot tubs and a butler. My dad said Las Vegas is the brightest city on Earth, like astronauts can see it from space. Isn't that cool?"

I couldn't risk telling Taryn Vegas sounded like the last place on earth I would ever want to go. I also didn't have the energy to ask if she even realized how much precious electricity the city wasted to keep an 80 foot cowboy lit up like a Christmas tree. My single focus was getting her to the swamp. This was a bad time for an argument. I was actually proud of myself for finally ignoring that voice, the one that wanted so badly to rip into her.

At the edge of the swamp, I coasted to a stop and laid my bike in a bed of button bush. From somewhere in the shadows a northern flicker could be heard rattling. As if our arrival signaled all the power and fury of a hurricane, the rusty brown tail of a brown thrasher could be seen wriggling its way into the safety of a wild rose bush.

The colors were magnificent. The purple of the phlox and oranges of the jewel weed made the swamp glow. It was also filled with a carnival of sound as the buzzing cicadas and furious drumming of a red headed woodpecker created a beautiful melody. Never before had the swamp seemed more alive to me than at that moment.

"Why're we stopping here?" Taryn asked, wrinkling her nose.

"This is the swamp," I explained, kicking my shoes off.

I was ankle deep in the murky water before noticing Taryn was still on her bike. "Yeah, and it's loaded with nasty mosquitoes and all kinds of…I don't know…creepy crawly stuff!" she choked. "What are you doing anyway? Why are you going in there? Be careful! Wow!" Taryn howled, pinching her nose. "What smells? Do you think there's radioactive material buried in there or something? Someone should put some signs up. I can't believe nobody has put a chain link fence around this thing yet!"

Creepy crawly stuff? Chain link fence? Is that really what she thought of the swamp? This was going to be harder than I'd imagined. What was she looking for after all? Who needed the bright lights of Vegas when you had water lotus and orange coneflowers?

"See these?" I said pointing at the muddy edge. "These little holes are where a woodcock has been probing the mud for worms."

"PEWWW! I can't wait till they get this place drained, what a stink hole!" She declared, turning her face away in disgust.

My own list of rules flashed through my head before I could say what I was really thinking. 'Agree with whatever they say…agree with whatever they say'. For once my brain was faster than my mouth.

"Yeah…" I choked, "it doesn't smell that great here. Hey, look over there," I pointed toward a row of trees. "See those boxes? Just above the yellow water lilies? There are families of woodies living there."

"Woodies?" Taryn repeated as if she were about to vomit.

"Wood ducks," I clarified, "but some call them tree ducks since that's where they live."

"And you know this why? I mean no offense, Kay, but talk about useless knowledge!"

Yeah, useless knowledge I repeated to myself. I wanted to tell Taryn how Grandpa Tug had taught me everything. I wanted to tell her that he used to bring me to this swamp almost every day in the summertime. I wanted to tell her how Grandpa Tug and I had hung those wood duck boxes just a few years ago.

If only she knew I could rattle off the Latin names of everything we saw. 'Aix sponsa' and 'Charadrius vociferus' and dozens more. For a moment I thought about mentioning the bulldozers and earthmovers lurking beyond the trees, but I resisted. Nothing could jeopardize 'Operation Cowbird'.

I even wished the Trash Queen were here. She would agree with me. She would tell Taryn how special this place was.

"Let's get out of here," Taryn implored. "It's hot and the bugs are so already eating me alive."

'Agree with whatever they say' flashed through my mind. "Yeah," I mumbled weakly, "they can be pretty bad…" All the while I was thinking, 'jeez, Stupid! There wouldn't be anything over here if the bugs were gone!' What do you think the flicker and cuckoo eat after all? Taryn was going to be a harder nut to crack than I thought.

"Let's go get some ice cream and hang out in the condo game room. It has air conditioning! And boys!!"

I stood in knee deep water staring across the swamp. A red-winged blackbird perched in the cattails was staring back at me. His beady little eyes were screaming, 'Get her out of here!'

"Yeah…air conditioning," I repeated slowly. I must have sounded like a robot. I didn't want to sit in the air conditioning. I wanted to cross the swamp and look for heron chicks. If only she knew their nests grew larger each year because they were reused. So large that anywhere from 6-12 families could live in the same tree forming a brood. Theirs was the original condo. One without air conditioning or boys. If only Grandpa Tug had taught Taryn that too.

How could anyone be surrounded by all this beauty and go on yammering about air conditioning and boys? My neck grew warm. She was just like her dad. He was always nattering on about knocking something down just to build something else.

Suddenly everywhere I looked I saw the lush green fescue of Art Guilafante's championship golf course. I saw fat, rich men smoking cigars and tossing empty beer cans into the heather. They would drive their golf carts over the ridge where the geese had built their nests. This would all change soon unless somebody stopped it. There were no two ways about it. Operation Cowbird had to work, or all this would soon be gone.

23

～～～～～～

Every time I felt good about Weird Harold being on my side, he would do something that made me question our partnership. Like biting into a deep fried Twinkie covered with gnats or digging in his yard at 3 am.

Now the pile of dirt in his back yard had swelled to the size of a small mountain. He'd been at it every night. Whir, klunk, shoosh. Whir, klunk, shoosh. Nonstop. I had no idea what Harold was doing back there, but whatever it was, he was committed to it.

I didn't have time to sort all that out now. Operation Cowbird was moving forward quickly. Kyle had done a good job of following my orders, which is to say he hadn't screwed anything up. We'd managed to keep Mom and Dad in the dark so far, and I'd even wadded a note up and thrown it over Harold's fence to let him know what our plan was.

My dad had been preoccupied and therefore out of the way. Of course he was still torn up about Grandpa's Toy sinking and us leaving him behind to sleep in the shed the night before. And not a second went by when he wasn't muttering about his sore leg or having to fix the shed door or the lookout tower or the rope swing, but I knew for Operation Cowbird to be a success, we had to move on without him.

Russell Guilafante had suggested a game of tag football, which Kyle and I, in sticking with my number four rule for winning the Guilafantes over, agreed to with wide smiles. I suggested boys versus girls, which would help Kyle and me bond better with Russ and Taryn.

The game didn't last long. Taryn broke a nail on the second play and we had to call a permanent time out. After lunch came rides on the Guilafante's jet skis. Kyle and I weren't allowed to ride them alone, but Abby was. Russell and Kyle worked on getting big air on their machine as Taryn and I just rode around in slow circles. Of course I hung on pretending to have the time of my life, but thinking all along how completely pointless it was to be riding aimlessly around in circles.

We finished the day eating some of Mrs. Guilafante's chocolate chip cookies together. I felt the need to add a "Gee, Mrs. G, these cookies are the tops!" To which Kyle responded a little too earnestly, "Yeah, I've never met more nicer people than you before. You are the nicest people I've ever known. How'd you get so nice? What's it like to be so nice? Do you take nice pills or something?"

While I'd be the first to admit Kyle was actually making a commendable effort at winning Betsy Guilafante over, I still kicked him under the table for laying it on too thick.

"Well, I just can't begin to tell you how happy we are to have such great neighbors at the lake!" Betsy beamed at us.

Great neighbors? I couldn't help but think that if this is what her husband did to 'great neighbors', I'd hate to see what he did to the ones he really didn't like.

"It's great to see you guys finally trying to get along with the neighbors!" Mom said later as we sat on the front deck sipping fresh lemonade. The thick smell of steaks sizzling on an outdoor grill hung in the air. From down the road came the thumping of bags on a cornhole board.

"I'm just really glad you've been able to move past all that nonsense about Art Guilafante trying to kill you. Now maybe you can just focus on having some fun," Dad said.

"You were right, Dad," I admitted, giving him my best 'don't look too close or you might realize I've got my fingers crossed behind my back' smile.

"Yeah, Dad. You're the smartest guy ever. Thank you for helping me see how stupid it was to think Art Guilafante wanted to kill us." Kyle continued apologizing, as if rehearsed, "I was stupid for believing Kay, and Kay was stupid for thinking Art was a bad guy. The whole thing was just plain stupid, and I want to thank both of you for helping us finally see our own stupidity. It never ceases to amaze me how wise you are."

I would have kicked him again, but he had strategically located himself out of my leg's reach. Still it was a marvel that, for all the movies he'd seen, my brother was such a tremendously bad actor. When the phone rang, Abby raced to answer it. She was beaming when she returned.

"Who was it, sweetie?"

"The Guilafantes."

"Really? Just calling to make sure we're all alive and okay?" I asked.

"No, apparently Russell and Taryn want Kyle and Kay to stay the night."

Operation Cowbird had worked. Kyle's face lit up and I saw his lips purse to say the words 'it worked', but before he could, the expression on my face made it clear that, if he did, I would kick him as hard as I could as soon as he was within reach of me.

No one had decorated Grandpa Tug's cottage since the 1950's. It was a cornucopia of garage sale bargains and outdoor life memorabilia. There were pictures of Grandpa Tug on hunting trips sandwiched between two sets of mounted whitetail antlers. If our cottage was considered 1900's décor, the Guilafante's would have been somewhere in the neighborhood of 2150.

In true Big A style, he had a television that took up half the wall. It was so large, the detectives on the show he was watching looked like real men investigating a crime in Art's living room. They were walking around a suspect's apartment, asking questions and looking for clues. They looked so official with their sharp cut suit jackets and notepads flipped open. I wanted to reach out to them. I needed their help.

The couches were leather, all four of them, and instead of an old flea-infested moose head like the one hanging in our cottage, the walls of Art's cottage were decorated with fancy artwork. Art's wife said something about them being "contemporary works from popular Chicago artists", whatever that meant.

On a table near the door was a picture of Betsy Guilafante. She was wearing a fur so large it looked like she was giving a piggy back ride to a 500 pound grizzly. The sight alone was enough to make me want to roll Art's wife up in a ball and rocket her back to the city with all the force of a Roni Bonafetti dodgeball.

The Big A went on forever about his precious cottage. How the floor had been laid in heated tile and the security system had been installed by the same company who did the White House. As he went on, my eyes fell on the Segway resting alone in the corner. It seemed fitting that such a large man with such a large ego and such a large pocketbook would feel it necessary to have a scooter to get around his tiny lake cottage.

Seeing all the new furniture and artwork reminded me of the way Grandpa Tug was always saying a lake cottage is the place where 'old furniture goes to die'. Seeing all the newfangled stuff the Guilafantes had brought to their lake cottage just confirmed what I'd believed all along; they weren't Bass Lake people.

We eventually sat down for a movie. Betsy Guilafante made everyone their own bowl of popcorn, with butter as thick as syrup layered throughout. For one brief moment, I actually felt comfortable. The thick buttery taste of the popcorn warmed my belly. It also helped me forget, for one brief moment that these people were trying to kill my family.

Taryn and Russ shared a bedroom with two sets of bunk beds on opposite walls. When the movie was over, Kyle and I climbed into ours as Russ and Taryn settled into theirs.

"What did you guys think of the movie?" Taryn asked.

"I liked it," I answered quickly.

"It was awesome, especially that one scene where the guys jumped their car over that burning house!" Russ said.

"I thought it was incredibly predictable," Kyle explained. "I mean the characters were totally flat and left a lot to be desired. The story seemed to wind around aimlessly, and so much of it was overly contrived. I mean the climax never really even had time to fully develop, but that's not a writing issue. That's on the director."

The room went silent as Russ and Taryn were left trying to gauge the full meaning of my brother's dorkness. I kicked hard at the top bunk.

"Yeah, sure, makes sense," Russ finally answered.

"Good night, you guys," Betsy Guilafante said, arriving in the doorway long enough to flip the lights off. "Blueberry pancakes in the morning!" she warbled while waltzing away down the hall.

The room grew quiet as we lay, just like two brown headed cowbirds lingering in an unsuspecting nest. The cottage was silent. The wind swept through the trees outside our window.

Suddenly my mind began racing. What were we doing? Art Guilafante had been trying to kill us for the better part of a week now, and my plan was to sleep in his house!? Suddenly Operation Cowbird seemed completely insane.

His old cottage was full of noises. Every creak I heard was Art Guilafante climbing the stairs. Every groan was him sawing away at a floor joist. Shadows moved along the wall outside my room as my heart began to race.

I closed my eyes. There was only one person I knew who would ever have been brave enough to sleep in Art Guilafante's cottage. "Grandpa Tug", I began softly, "I know you can't come back, but I also know you're up there and can hear me. Please keep Art from wrecking Bud and Ella's nest again…and oh yeah, from killing us too, and if you have some extra time, please try to convince Mom to buy some of that buttered popcorn like Art's wife made. It was really good. Thanks, G'pa."

Outside a car with a bad muffler could be heard struggling down Lake Road. As the sound of the car faded, my ears picked up something altogether different. It wasn't a creak or groan from the old cottage. It wasn't the cicadas outside or a faraway loon out on the water. Instead my heart surged upon hearing the voices of two men. Two men talking downstairs.

There it was again. That part of me I had such a hard time ignoring. It was at it again. Nagging me the way it always does. This time instead of a witty comeback or cheeky remark, it was telling me to get up, to get up out of my bed and find out what the two men downstairs were up to.

Once again, as had happened every other time before, I just couldn't say no.

Eric Walker Williams

24

~~~~~~

"Kyle, do you hear that!?" I whispered.

There was no response from the top bunk. The voices continued, but I couldn't understand them. They were too muffled.

"What is it?" he asked, half asleep.

"There are people talking downstairs. Let's go see who it is."

"We'll do it first thing tomorrow."

Right, first thing in the morning. Before I could yell at him, another voice was heard coming from outside. "Dang you Tricky!"

It was my dad's, and it was followed by the clanging of an aluminum garbage can. Then came a dull sound like that of a sandbag being dropped to the ground. I could only suspect this was the sound of my father falling over. "I'll get you one of these days!" he screamed.

As bad as I felt for my dad at that moment, there wasn't time to help him now. I had my own problems. For starters, Operation Cowbird was working perfectly, but now I didn't know what to do. Was I really going to get out of this bed and spy on Art Guilafante? The same Art Guilafante who looked like he could probably pick a bull elephant up and spin him on his finger like a basketball?

Even if I found a way to ignore that voice in my head, there was no guarantee I was going to walk out of this cottage in one piece. We'd survived so much to get to this point, why hadn't I just given up and asked Dad to sell the cottage? Trying to prove our neighbor was a killer suddenly seemed like the worst idea in the history of the world. Maybe my best move was to forget the whole thing and go back to bed. In the morning I could convince Mom and Dad to pack the car up and go home. That seemed the easiest way out of this mess.

Then came a noise from outside the window that I will never forget for my entire life. A noise so shrill and unsettling, yet so warm and welcome. It was the trilling of a screech owl. Low and rising, it sounded like the high pitched whinny of a horse. The sound filled my lungs with a new breath. I could feel courage pooling inside me now. Of all things to hear at that moment, it had been a screech owl. There had been so many nights Grandpa Tug and I had sat listening for them in the swamp. More than any other, we loved to hear their spooky calls. I could feel it in my legs again, the heavy skis, the rope in my hands. 'Sit on the chair, sit on the chair.' This was the sign I'd asked for. The sign Grandpa Tug was watching and wanted me to get out of bed.

I was thinking more quickly now as I sat up. "Kyle, act like you're talking in your sleep." I whispered, "We need to be sure Russ and Taryn are sleeping."

"I'd like to thank the Academy for this award..." he declared softly, his voice reflecting the fact he was lost somewhere deep inside a dream. The rest of his acceptance speech was soon buried by heavy snoring.

"Kyle!" I snapped quietly. "Wake up already! I need your help!"

My brother snorted and snarled for a moment, shifting his bed. I laid still, hoping Kyle was about to rise from his slumber. Soon enough his snoring filled the room again, so I threw my covers off and crept to the top of the stairs.

Stopping at the bannister overlooking the downstairs, I peered down into a dimly lit room. The shadow of the Big A sitting on his couch was unmistakable. The other figure had his back turned to me.

"We're awful close," Art announced.

"Close only counts in horseshoes and hand grenades, Art." the man on the couch answered. There was a stern tone in his voice, as if he were unhappy.

"We just need these last two cottages," the Big A explained, dropping his finger on the blueprints sprawled across his coffee table. "Then we'll be able to go ahead with the plans."

"Of course, but how can we be sure they'll sell?"

"What did I tell you the first time we met?" Art asked.

I didn't need to hear it, I knew what was coming. Art was going to tell the man 'Everything has a price'.

"I've talked to them face to face, Art. They don't sound like they're willing to sell."

"They'll sell," Art guaranteed. "Just as sure as that mustache of yours will still have a curl in it when you wake up in the morning. They'll sell. Trust me, I'll make sure of it."

My heart almost stopped. There was only one man on the lake who had a mustache with a curl. Art Guilafante was talking to the President of Bass Lake! Weird Harold had been right. The answer did lie in the blueprints. The Big A's plans did include our cottage.

I shuddered as Art's words spun wildly through my mind, 'They'll sell. Trust me, I'll make sure of it.' Suddenly I couldn't shake the thought of Big Art Guilafante's big hands reaching for my throat. I saw his big hands sawing the rope limb, the garage door supports, the look out tower legs. I didn't need to hear anymore. Scrambling to my feet, I hurried back to the bedroom.

We had to get out of Art's cottage as quickly as possible. I dashed to Kyle's bunk. Before I could wake him up, someone had turned the hall light on. In a flash I dove into the bottom bunk. Before I could even think about covering myself with any blankets there was a loud snapping noise.

I'd heard it before. On the rope swing, in the shed, running down the lookout tower. I looked up in time to find the top bunk, and my brother Kyle, falling down on top of me. The weight instantly crushed me into my mattress. Everything went dark and quiet. The world was filled by the sounds of creaking bed springs.

Was I dead? Was this what it was like? Did heaven smell like a musty featherbed? There wasn't a sliver of light to be found. Was I inside a coffin? Then I heard my brother snoring. Somehow he'd slept through the whole thing.

Before anyone could move, the Big A flipped the light switch on in the bedroom.

"What the devil?" he cursed over the shattered bed. "Are you two all right?" Art raised the bed off of me. My leg was throbbing, and I could feel another large scrape across my forehead. I was in pain, but it mattered little. This was it. My life was over. As terrible as that thought was, at least somehow I knew I would die safe in the knowledge that I'd been right about Art Guilafante all along.

Eric Walker Williams

The Big A looked like he was ready to pound me against the bunk beds, kingfisher-style. I closed my eyes to brace for the end. If he didn't pound me against the bed, what would be his choice of weapon? A knife? An axe? A club? Maybe he'd use his blueprint tube or a hand mixer. I hoped against the hand mixer, for that sounded like a long, painful, and quite messy death.

"What's going on?" another voice asked as Wilbert Harley arrived at the doorway and peered his round head inside.

That's when I did it. There wasn't any time for planning or to think it through. It honestly kind of just happened. It was one of those moments where you react without thinking. Instinct just takes over, and you do what you think will help keep you alive at that moment.

That was the moment I screamed, and it wasn't your garden variety, 'Oh I saw a spider run across my shoe' kind of scream. This was undoubtedly a 'My freakishly large and incredibly obnoxious neighbor is trying to kill me' kind of scream. In fact, my scream rang out as an eardrum piercing caterwaul unlike anything ever heard before on Bass Lake. It was on a frequency somewhere between nails on a chalkboard and that dog whistle humans can't hear.

Like a flash of lightning, my scream shot out the window of the cottage and rocketed its way across the lake. It was a scream that was so loud I'm sure somewhere outside even Weird Harold had to stop giving people the stink eye long enough to cover his ears. It was so loud I felt quite certain the heron mothers were cowering over their nests in the swamp.

The air was barely out of my lungs when my dad appeared in the doorway standing in his pajamas. "What happened up here!?"

"It's happening again!!" I yelled.

"What's happening?" the President responded anxiously.

All eyes were locked on me; Russ and Taryn, the President, Art, and my dad. I'm certain Kyle would have been looking at me too except he was somehow still sound asleep. Everyone was staring at me. Suddenly I couldn't speak. My heart was racing so fast I didn't know where to start. Without speaking a word I raised my hand and pointed an incriminating finger at Art Guilafante and said the five words I had been fighting back all week.

Five words so bold and so powerful they shocked everyone in the room, and told Art Guilafante exactly what I had been suspecting all week.

Eric Walker Williams

25

~~~~~~

"**H**e's trying to kill us?" Dad repeated my words over his plate of eggs. "Of all the things to say to your neighbor you chose those. Not, 'Hey, the lawn looks great' or 'Hey, thanks for keeping an eye on the place while we were gone'. No, you chose, 'He's trying to kill us'."

Coming from my father at eight thirty in the morning, the words sounded completely ridiculous. In fact, they sounded almost insane.

"Yeah, Kay, I wish you would have told me you were going to say that. That would have been an amazing shot to have for *The Curse of Bass Lake.*"

"I thought you were past all this!?" Dad asked, massaging the vein on his forehead.

"Before we get too far into all this again, can I just say how well that headwrap compliments your eyes? It really draws out the blue," Abby said of the bandages Mom had placed on my head after I'd successfully caught Kyle's collapsing bunk with my face.

"You look like one of those fortune tellers from the movies, you know like Madam Bardo or something," Kyle said.

"Thanks, Kyle, and can I just say once again thanks for falling asleep and not waking up at all when I was yet again almost killed!"

"You're lucky you didn't break your leg!" Mom shrieked.

"I don't get it. If you don't trust Art Guilafante, why would you agree to spend the night in his house?" Dad asked.

"It was our plan," Kyle confessed. "Well, Kay's plan really."

I kicked my brother under the table so hard he came up out of his seat. "Plan?" Mom repeated in shock. "You had a *plan?*"

The room fell silent. Outside the shish, shish, shish of Art's lawn sprinkler could be heard.

"We were going to be nice to the Guilafantes and hope they invited us over to spend the night. That way we could get a look at Art's blueprints. Kay called it Operation Cow Turd," Kyle answered, bouncing in his seat as I kicked him again.

"It was cowbird, you half-wit, Operation Cowbird."

"Blueprints?" My parents repeated in unison.

"The blueprints Harold told us about," Kyle explained, jerking his knees to his chest quickly, so I couldn't 'say hello' to them again.

"Harold!?" My dad squawked, "You've been talking to Harold again?"

I nodded as if giving Harold and all his weirdness my seal of approval.

"I never realized my children were so," my dad began as the life in his eyes seemed to fade. For once he seemed to be at a total loss for words.

"So scheming, so deceitful, so slippery, so manipulating, so plotting, and so distrustful?" Mom answered, in what I could only guess was a tremendous effort at finishing my dad's thought.

Art Guilafante had not taken it well when I accused him of trying to kill us. His face just kind of got all red before he said something about it being time for us to go. Still, I felt lucky Dad showed up when he did. There was no telling what Art and the President would have done to us.

"I have video of Art, Dad. Proof that he messed with Grandpa's Toy!"

"Oh just stop with your nonsense already."

"Just look at my camera! I have it all on video!"

"I should have thrown that thing off the wall when I had the chance," growled my dad.

"But what about the bed?" Kyle shrieked. "How's come our bed collapsed and not Russ and Taryn's? Don't you see what's going on here?"

Dad didn't answer. His thoughts were lost in blueprints and bandages. Everything was unraveling. We had agreed to keep it all to ourselves, and now Kyle was cracking under the pressure. As long as my brother had kicked the door wide open, I thought I might as well step in.

"That's not all," I began. Another hush fell over the room as all eyes rolled toward me. "I heard something while I was there."

Nobody spoke. It grew so quiet, the crunching of Kyle's Corn Flakes began shaking the cottage walls.

"What did you hear?" Abby asked anxiously.

"I heard the Big A talking to the President," I answered sharply. "The very same President who was standing on our front porch just three days ago asking about buying the cottage."

The room fell silent again. Mom froze, her coffee mug suspended in front of her face.

Kyle froze, his cheeks so full of Corn Flakes he looked like a chipmunk getting ready for winter.

"They were talking about the lake."

Eyes darted about the room as we found ourselves sharing one of those moments where everyone knows exactly what the other is thinking, but nobody actually wants to say it. It was just like the time Grammie Minnie gave my Dad a membership to the 'Tie of the Month Club'. We all knew he hated it, but there was no way anybody was going to tell Grammie that.

"And what did they say about the lake?" Mom pressed.

"They said they needed two more cottages to sell before they could go ahead with their plans."

"Two more cottages?" Abby choked.

"Plans?" Kyle choked, Corn Flakes exploding from his mouth like candy from a piñata.

"Yeah, but that's not all," I continued as Kyle was busy raking soggy Corn Flakes off the table and back into his bowl, "the President kept saying he didn't think the last two would ever sell."

"As in our cottage and Harold's!" Kyle answered quickly.

My mind flashed to the night we'd arrived. The strange way Weird Harold had told us he would never sell his cottage. It was almost like he had known what was going to happen all along. There was no way around it. The Minnix and Farcus cottages *had* to be the last two the President and Art were talking about.

I looked at my dad. His elbows were propped on the table, both hands busy massaging the bulging vein in his head.

"I knew he was after us all along!" Kyle declared.

"You did not!" I snarled. "You liked all his stuff! You liked the jet skis, his Too-Big-For- Bass-Lake-Floatplane. Heck, you even rode the Segway in his living room!"

"He has a Segway in his living room?" Mom asked, doing a poor job of hiding the fact she was impressed.

Eric Walker Williams

"All right, that's enough! Everyone calm down!" my dad said, waving his arms around in a manner that exuded anything but calm. "This is our last day at the lake. We're going home first thing in the morning, and I'm not going to sit around the cottage while my children try to build a federal case against Art Guilafante. I will admit some strange things have happened this week, but I am not willing to admit under *any* circumstances that anyone is actually out to scare my family off the lake."

Dad parked his coffee cup on the counter before tossing his plate in the sink. "Everybody get cleaned up. We're going in to town today. Its festival weekend, and we're going to find something to do that will help you forget all this Art Guilafante garbage."

"Speaking of garbage dear," Mom started, her eyes gazing out the kitchen window in the direction of the driveway. "Who's going to clean up Tricky's mess this morning?"

Dad braced himself on the kitchen counter with both hands, his face racked with anger. I knew exactly what he was thinking. In his mind, he was out on the lake under a bright summer sun, not a care in the world, waterskiing happily in his new coonskin cap.

On our way into town we passed by the old drive-in. The windows on the ticket booth were boarded up. Just seeing the place reminded me of Grandpa Tug. He was always talking about the 'good ol' days'. Days when they still gave free pony rides at the drive-in-theatre and church services were held there on Sundays, days when your neighbors didn't want to kill you.

The trip took us past Art Guilafante's new condos. A towering billboard in front of the construction site featured a picture of the Big A's face. Sporting one of his giant cheesy smiles, Art was pointing at a set of his new plastic condos. The words 'Bass Lake: A family lake' were scribbled across his chest.

A family lake? He'd stolen that line from my dad. Art believed Bass Lake was a family lake about as much as I believed Vegas was a great place to take your children.

"Barf," I muttered under my breath as our car wheeled past.

We ate lunch at Mr. Happy Burger's diner before walking down Main Street to the theatre. Evidently my dad's grand plan for forgetting Art Guilafante included going to the movies. This sounded like a solid idea until we saw the letters across the marquee announcing the one and only feature:

THE KILLER NEXT DOOR

"What do you think?" Dad asked, the tone in his voice suggesting he was actually entertaining the idea of seeing the movie.

Eric Walker Williams

Nobody answered, but together we pressed on. Along Main Street, vendors were hawking Bass Lake Festival t-shirts and wristbands. Abby was thrilled after scoring a pair of knock off sunglasses while Kyle won a five-foot-long stuffed bass at the milk ring toss. Of course none of this helped me forget what was going on. We'd reached a point of no return. The only thing that would make me happy was seeing the tail of Art Guilafante's floatplane leaving Bass Lake.

26

~~~~~~~

B y the time we returned to our cottage, the sun was setting on the wreck that used to be Grandpa Tug's lookout. The limb from the rope swing was still lying near shore
in the grass, and it was hard to ignore the doorless shed as we
pulled in the drive.

With the unmistakable signs of disaster and near fatal
accidents surrounding us, it was impossible to forget the way
Art Guilafante had haunted us for a week. It didn't matter
where you turned. Whether it was his Too-Big-For-Bass-
Lake-Floatplane or the collapsed look out, his plastic condos
or earthmoving equipment or the billboards, the one man I
hated more than any other in the world had his fingerprints
all over the one place I loved more than any other in the
world.

Everyone hurried into the cottage as if escaping a
storm, everyone except Dad who was still fighting a limp.
I stopped on the deck to glance back at the water. Bud and
Ella were flying in their circles. Nobody was after them. They
didn't have to worry about their world collapsing around
them. They seemed happy, which was the way the lake had
always made me feel before I met Art Guilafante.

Once inside, Abby spun all three locks on our front door. "Let's all just get our things packed up and be ready to leave first thing in the morning," Mom said softly.

There was no response. Everyone just stood motionless in the living room, lifeless expressions on our faces. Art Guilafante had won. We were running away. My stomach began twisting in two directions at once. Part of me wanted to run away, to go back to Chicago and resume the life I knew. The one where monsters in designer shades weren't lurking behind every door.

But the Grandpa Tug part of me wanted to stay at the lake and fight for our cottage, our way of life. This was the part I was used to listening to, but the more I thought about everything we'd been through, the more I realized how lucky I was to still be alive. In fact, the more I thought about it, the more I became convinced leaving was best.

Before anyone could start packing up, a knock on the door rattled the cottage walls. Strange glances were exchanged, as if each were daring the other to open the door. Knock...knock...knock. Finally my mom lost her patience and made her way to the door. Slowly it fell open. The shrieking hinges soon gave way to the same thundering voice I'd grown so accustomed to hearing over the past week. A harbinger of trouble.

"Hey there Kathy!" Art Guilafante beamed from our front porch. With his family flanking him, the Big A's outstretched hand was offering a bottle of wine. "I just thought since I almost killed your children last night, we should try to make it up to you!"

My mom reluctantly accepted the bottle as Art and his family forced their way into our cottage. "It's a Riesling from the 1920's," Art explained, running his hands along the wood paneled walls of our living room. "I'm sorry if you don't like it, but it's all we had in the house."

Art went on working his way down the wall, knocking on the paneling as if testing its quality or looking for a hidden wall safe.

"Honey, the Guilafantes are here," Mom announced in a tone that was about a million miles away from enthused.

"He says he wants to apologize for trying to kill us," I explained, my voice filled with the bravado of knowing I'd been right all along.

Art had no reaction. Instead he turned away from the wall he'd been inspecting and grabbed the bottle from Mom's hands. "Well, come on now, let's pop the cork on this thing. It's not every day you get to share a $400 bottle of wine with friends. Am I right, Walt?"

"Kids," Mom started, "why don't you take Russ and Taryn upstairs and show them your rooms?"

When none of us moved, Mom gave us her look. It was the same, 'I'm not telling you again, young lady' look she was always giving Abby. While it never seemed to faze Abby, Kyle and I weren't teenagers yet, so it was enough to prod us upstairs.

Kyle led the way with Russ and Taryn in tow. While everyone hustled to our bedroom, I stopped at the top of the stairs and knelt down behind the banister where nobody could see me.

"Well, since you're here and all, I just want to tell you how sorry I am for what Kayla said to you last night. I mean as a mother I'm horrified that a child of mine could ever be so rude."

"Don't sweat it, Kathy. If I had a dollar for every ridiculous thing my kids have said, I'd be a rich man. Well, you know, I mean more rich than I am now, of course."

"Anyway, Kathy," Art's wife began. "That's not why we're here at all. Art and I just feel so terrible for all you've been through this past week, and well, we've decided we'd like to offer to have Art's construction company come down and repair everything."

"At half cost of course," the Big A added with a wink. The man smiled as if he thought offering half price was more than enough to make up for the fact he'd been trying to kill his neighbors for an entire week now.

"Oh, I don't know, Betsy. It's very generous of you, but we're not really even sure what we're going to do with this place yet."

"Here we go," my dad said, carrying a tray of juice glasses and a bottle opener into the room.

"Well, you're not thinking about selling are you?" The Big A asked.

The question hit my dad so hard he nearly dropped his tray. Two glasses slid off as the sound of glass shattering on the hardwood floor ricocheted off the walls of the cottage.

"Oh, Walter!" Mom blared.

"Bad case of two left feet there, Walt?" The Big A chuckled.

I felt like shoving my foot in Art's mouth for laughing at my dad. I'd like to see how well that big knucklehead could get around if Russell had kneecapped him with a baseball bat.

Another knock on the door came as Dad knelt down to clean the glass shards from the floor. Mom only had the door halfway open before Wilbert Harley pushed his way in. The rotund little politician was wearing a bright red shirt that read: 'President of Bass Lake-Wilbert Harley-Democrat'.

The arrival of the President turned my neck warm. A soft breeze was coming through the window at the top of the stairs, but it was doing little to cool me down. Since the cottage had no air conditioning, the windows were always left open in the summer time. Grandpa Tug had never installed screens either, relying on only thin, eyelet curtains to keep the insects out.

Through the fluttering curtain I saw Weird Harold sitting in his white plastic lawn chair outside. He looked innocent enough, but I knew he was trying his best to eavesdrop through the open window. However, even Weird Harold, strange as he was, would not believe the bizarre series of events that were about to unfold inside the Minnix family cottage.

27

~~~~~~

"You must be Walter!" the President said, ramming his squat hand into my father's palm. "Wilbert Harley-President of Bass Lake. Nice to meet you!"

"Looks like we'll need five glasses, dear," Mom announced, surrendering to good manners.

"Just thought I'd stop by," Wilbert Harley said, sinking into our couch, "since I've never met you folks and all."

"Well, how nice of you to invite yourself over!" Mom answered, her voice so full of sarcasm she sounded like an owner telling her pet, 'Well, it was so very nice of you to lift your leg and pee all over the new couch!'

"Well, you know that's one thing I've learned about this old lake through the years," the President explained. "One's cottage door is always open!"

"As long as it doesn't collapse into a pile of dust," I muttered from the top of the stairs.

After Art Guilafante finished pouring wine for everyone in the room, nobody spoke. An uncomfortable silence lingered as eyes darted about. Somewhere the chortle of a red bellied woodpecker was heard.

I wasn't sure what to do next. Looking down the hall I could see the Queen of Hormonestan lying on her bed, head bobbing back and forth as she listened to music. She was mumbling the words to some silly pop song, headphones in her ears.

I was out of ideas. For some reason, the voice in my head was telling me the Queen would know what to do, so I headed for her room. As I hit the doorway, a hairy brown blob fell through Abby's window and landed on the bed behind her. It was Tricky. I screamed, but my sister couldn't hear me.

What happened next remains somewhat of a blur, because it began with our cottage in one piece and ended with it as an absolute disaster. In a flash, Tricky had scurried up my sister's legs, and climbed her back before using her head as a springboard to launch himself into the air. With an angry thirty-five-pound raccoon flying toward me as if it had discovered the secret to flight, I scrambled for cover.

Soon enough, Abby's screams were filling the cottage as the rat-a-tat-tat of Tricky's paws on the hardwood fired after me down the hall. I sprinted for the top of the stairs where my feet hit one of Grammie Minnie's old throw rugs. Sliding across the floor I was transformed into a surfer riding a wave. For one small moment I was alone, my own spectacular tube ride, until I realized my point break was going to be the banister at the top of the stairs.

Crashing into it, the banister broke away from the wall as if it were made of toothpicks and Elmer's glue. My body followed the railing as we both began tumbling through the air over the living room. Spinning like a trapeze artist in the circus, I fell from the second floor before landing safely on the lap of Art Guilafante.

Kyle stood at the top of the stairs with Russ and Taryn, training his camera down the hall in the direction of Abby's room.

"Here he comes!!" Taryn screamed.

What followed next was that all too familiar groan I'd come to know so well. The one that sounded like an old man climbing from his chair after being roused from a nap. A loud clap of thunder rang out as the upstairs landing tore away from the wall. Plaster and wood rained down from the ceiling as the upper half of the staircase began falling to the floor.

A storm of wood shards, plaster dust, and planks rained down on the living room as Russ, Taryn and Abby tumbled to the floor together. Meanwhile, Kyle rocketed through the air as if he'd been thrown by the golden arm of Roni Bonafetti herself. At some point his body twisted into a full somersault as his hand let go of his camera. Kyle landed on the coffee table with a thud before his camera met the wall and instantly exploded into a thousand pieces. With his son lying on the coffee table covered from head to toe with plaster, Dad's eyes became filled with satisfaction while gazing upon the spot on the wall that had destroyed Kyle's camera.

Before anyone could speak, the table he was lying on collapsed under Kyle's weight. The collapse sent a thunderous vibration up the wall and shook Grandpa Tug's prized moose head loose from its mount. That magnificent creature, with its spectacular six-foot-wide rack and impressive dewlap, fell conveniently into Betsy Guilafante's lap, causing her to scream and toss her glass of wine skyward.

There was a pause as everyone was busy processing all that had happened. This was broken by the shattering of Betsy Guilafante's glass on the hardwood floor. Overhead, the patter of Tricky's little paws could be heard. They scurried from the house quickly, but not before we could all detect what sounded like a faint snicker coming from the wily raccoon.

"Art! Save me, Art! Save me!" Betsy Guilafante began wheezing like a weed eater, her legs flailing wildly under the weight of the moose head. For one magical moment, the Queen of Capitalism, with her three-hundred-dollar alligator purses, Tahitian pearls, and Siberian lynx coat sat nose to nose with that hairy beast before fainting.

That's when I remembered whose lap I was in. Wrestling myself free of the Big A, I stood up to point a finger at him. "How convenient!" I howled. "What're the odds this would happen while you two are here!?"

"What do you mean?" the President responded, his little round face balled up in confusion.

"I've had enough of this!" I snapped back. "You're not going to be happy until one of us is gone are you? And for what? All for some stupid old cottage? Is it really worth killing someone?"

Nobody answered me. Slowly the Big A's mouth began to crank open, and little by little it grew, until it became so large it looked like the clown's mouth people shoot water through at the county fair.

I was on the edge of my seat, waiting for the monster's response, when a loud knock was heard at the door. Mom stepped over what was left of the staircase and some random chunks of plaster from the ceiling to answer the door.

When it fell open, the Sheriff of California County was waiting outside. With a wide brimmed hat tucked under his arm, the man stepped into the house. As if expected, he tucked his free thumb inside his gun belt.

My heart leapt. The police were involved now. This was getting serious. Who was he after? Was he here to arrest the Big A? Was he here to arrest me for accusing the Big A? Was he here because Art had turned me in for snooping in his shed? Was he here to arrest Wilbert Harley for impersonating the President of the United States? Could this be about Alison Camarillo copying my math homework in third grade?

"Did someone here ring the law?" He asked, gazing over the disaster that was our living room. His face projected no reaction. Somehow, he seemed oblivious to the fact it looked like a nuclear bomb had exploded inside our cottage.

Nobody answered. Eyes darted back and forth. I looked at Mom, Mom looked at Dad. Dad looked at the President who swung his little round head toward the Big A. Art's face was blank as he turned to his wife who was still out cold with Grandpa Tug's moose head resting in her lap.

"Is he all right?" The Sheriff asked, pointing at my brother, who was lying motionless on the coffee table with so much dust and plaster covering him that he looked like an Egyptian mummy.

The room was spinning. Art Guilafante had become so determined to get us that he didn't even care about destroying the cottage he so desperately wanted. I didn't know what to do. For some reason, my mind jumped to Bud and Ella. How Art had torn their nest down and fought them at every turn. He'd tried so hard to run those two off, yet they always just kept coming back.

They were resilient. Suddenly I was waterskiing with Grandpa Tug again. So many times I'd quit so easily. There hadn't been a single resilient bone in my body. It made me sick inside. Grandpa had asked me to hang on, asked me to give it another chance, but I had walked away.

The time had come. I had survived everything Art had thrown at me to this point. I wasn't about to walk away now. A resilient person doesn't give up in the face of failure. A resilient person finds a way to press on when things get tough. A resilient person would have hung on to that rope and let the boat drag her across the lake.

This had gone on long enough. It was time to be resilient. So with the Sheriff standing in our living room, I found the courage to grab that rope. To clench it in my fists and force myself to stand up. I drew in a deep breath, and with as much force as I could muster, said the first thing that came to my mind. "Sheriff, I want to report a murder!"

28
~~~~~~~

The word 'murder' hung in the air. Had I really just said
it? Did I really mean it? Nobody had died. How could I
report a murder? I knew murder was a really strong word but
I felt it necessary to fully illustrate everything Art Guilafante
had done.

"A murder?" the Sheriff repeated, his hand switching to
his pistol nervously.

"Well, not a real murder... more of an almost murder...a series of attempts, really."

"She means an attempted murder," Kyle groaned, still
lying motionless on what was left of our coffee table.

"Okay, look. The weird guy in the hat next door flagged
me down. He said he thought there was trouble in here, and
judging by this mess, he's right. But as far as murder goes,
well, I'm sorry miss, you're going to have to be a little more
clear," the law man answered.

"Art Guilafante tried to kill us!" I shouted leveling my
finger at the man.

My dad's palm slammed over his face as he fell back
into the couch. "What!?" the Big A gasped, a look of disbelief
cresting his face.

"Don't you *what* me!" my voice grated. "You know what you did! You cut the limb to our rope swing, and you cut the supports for the garage door. You cut the stairs on the look-out and drilled a hole in Grandpa's Toy!"

"And you made *our* bunk collapse instead of Russ and Taryn's," Kyle growled, though nobody could see his face for the white plaster covering it.

"And pulled our stairwell loose from the wall so that it would fall down as well. Look at it!" I pointed at the pile of debris that used to be our stairs, just in case there was somebody left in the room who didn't realize part of our cabin had collapsed.

"Arrest him!" I howled, pointing at Art.

"Yeah! What do you have to say for yourself now, Guilafante?" Kyle asked.

"Be careful," Abby began, "In Miranda vs. Arizona the Supreme Court decided that an arresting police officer must make their suspect fully aware of their fifth and sixth amendment rights prior to taking them into custody. Failure to do so renders said suspect's testimony inadmissible in a U.S. court of law."

Everyone stopped to look at my sister as if those were the first words she had ever spoken in her life, instead of just the most intelligent. There was no response from the Sheriff. He just stood back trying to make sense of it all, tugging at his gun belt as if unsure of what to do next. "Mr. Guilafante," he started softly. "You don't have to listen to this. If they want to file a complaint, I can hang around and take it down."

"That's alright, Sheriff," Art answered, standing up. He turned toward me, his big wide eyes narrowing, "Actually, I came over here today to mend some fences. I wanted to tell you how sorry I was to see that all these bad things were happening to you. I was going to offer to help you rebuild…I was even ready to buy the cottage from you if you just wanted to get rid of it."

Kyle finally moved, rising like a mummy coming back to life, "Frankly, my dear, I don't give a ham," he said.

Everyone in the room stopped to look at my brother. It was a quote he'd used before and one Dad insisted he clean up if he ever planned on using it again.

"You wanted to buy our cottages all right, ours and Weird Harold's!" I answered sharply.

"Kayla Marie! I told you to stop calling him that!" my mom snapped. "What happens if he hears you? Then what?"

"Then he'll know we think he's weird?" Kyle repeated.

"I heard you and the President talking about it last night! These two cottages were the last ones you needed to complete your plans!" I threw a pair of air quotes over 'complete your plans' just to be sure everyone knew I had heard them using those exact words.

The Big A stood rock still. I had him just where I wanted him. Now it was time to watch him sweat. This was the moment I'd been waiting for all week. The instant all my work was going to pay off.

But that's when, instead of sweat, I saw a huge smile crest the man's lips. "Well, I guess I understand now," he began softly. "What you heard was Wilbert and me talking about two cottages on the other side of the lake. We need to secure them to free up more parking space for the new condos."

My chest sank. Suddenly it felt like the walls of the cottage were collapsing around me. I tried to make sense of what Art was saying. Could I have been wrong? Was this the wild goose chase my dad had said it was all along? It was a jigsaw puzzle that seemed to fit together so perfectly. How could this be?

All the things Weird Harold had said came rushing back to me. The stuff about Jimmy Longstockings and his tree, his dog, and the magazines. My thoughts were racing so fast my mouth could barely keep up. "What about the guy next door? Jimmy Longstockings? Remember him? What about his dog? You wanted to buy his cottage and he said no and then his poor dog disappeared! What happened to him? Nobody saw him move out. And what about all his stuff? Why's it *still* in your shed?"

Art's face went blank. He didn't know I'd been in his shed, that much was clear. Maybe I shouldn't have admitted to it considering the Sheriff of California County was standing less than five feet away from me.

"Mr. Guilafante," the Sheriff said. "You don't have to answer to any of this."

"It's okay, Carl," the President said, raising a pudgy hand at the Sheriff. "I think I can explain part of this. Jimmy was moving to Florida. His wife hated the winters up here and she just couldn't keep up with all the work having a cottage takes. Before he left, he asked me to keep Checkers because his condo board in Sarasota doesn't allow dogs."

I pursed my lips to respond, but Kyle jumped in first, "So why did you stop by the other day and offer to buy our cottage?"

The Sheriff's steely eyes rolled toward the pudgy little president. Wilbert Harley's face went white as his fat little hand nervously stroked his curled mustache. All ears were trained on him, even Kyle's, which were filled with so much plaster he could barely hear.

Eric Walker Williams

"Well...," the President cleared his throat nervously, "I guess I came over here because of all the construction. The bulldozers and their gurgling motors, the pounding of the dump trucks and the screeching air brakes, the annoying beep-beep-beep when they back up. The far side just hasn't been the most peaceful place to live this summer, not as peaceful as it once was anyway."

I didn't feel sympathy for the President, not after he had been at our cottage rambling on and on about how great progress was.

"And," Wilbert Harley continued, staring at the floor as if disgusted with himself, "progress is great and all, but it didn't take me long to realize I didn't want to be near the condos when those rich city folks came in. I just wanted to be on this side of the lake. You know, it's just so much quieter over here. It was selfish of me, I know. I wanted to be here with the families. I wanted to live the way we always have up here. I also knew there was no way Farcus would ever sell, so I was curious if your parents might be interested. Heck, I asked everyone on this side if they were going to sell. Even old Art here."

"Wilbert came to me the other day, right after he'd talked to you kids on the porch," Art explained. "He asked me if I would be willing to sell, and I told him-"

"Everything has a price," I choked out softly.

All this time I'd had a fire burning in my belly to catch the Big A red-handed. To prove my father wrong. To prove my theory Art Guilafante was out to get us. Now the fire was fading fast as my carefully crafted theory was being doused by reality.

"You're right. Everything does have a price tag, but his wasn't high enough!" the Big A winked.

"Art, there's obviously been a huge misunderstanding here and I'm sorry," I heard my dad saying after he had peeled his hand from his face.

"That's okay, Walt. Despite all this, I still like your daughter's moxie," the big man answered.

It was all slipping away. The case I'd so carefully crafted was now spiraling down the drain. Kyle's video was too grainy. We couldn't put Art at any of the accidents before they happened. And the President had explained away key parts of our argument. All our work seemed lost. And then, what came next was perhaps the most unexpected of all. Art swung his big face in my direction and continued, "Just so you know, I also came over here today because I wanted to tell you I've decided to set aside some land for a wildlife preserve on the far side of the lake."

Who was this man pretending to be Art Guilafante? Why wasn't he being loud and laughing about tearing something down to build something else? Why wasn't he telling everyone wildlife refuges don't make money?

For the first time in a week the Big A looked human to me. His eyes seemed warm, his big hands looked soft, and his face wore a pained expression. "Taryn told me how you rode over there the other day and showed her the shorebirds. She couldn't stop talking about how beautiful they were, and it's just, well you need passion to make it in this world," Art explained taking a knee in front of me. "Taryn could tell you had a lot of passion for the animals on this lake, so we're going to set aside some of the land on the far side to make a nature preserve. It will include the area those rookeries are located in and the marsh where you and your grandfather put up the wood duck houses."

"But wildlife refuges..." I stammered. "don't make money."

"No, they don't, but let's just say, maybe through all this you taught me there are some things you can't put a price tag on," Art answered. Suddenly his big eyes seemed soft and watery.

"Anybody else think ordering a pizza sounds like a good idea right now?" Mom asked, trying to lighten the mood with food in the way only she could.

Suddenly I felt ridiculous. How could I have thought this man wanted to kill me? This kind, gentle, giant of a man. He was nothing more than a six foot seven teddy bear.

"So I guess there won't be anyone pressing any charges here?" the Sheriff asked no one in particular while tugging his hat on. He turned to walk out the door. "Give me a call if anyone changes their mind."

"General elections are in November," the President announced on his way out. He stopped to pat my dad on the shoulder as if nothing had happened. "Being that you live in the city and all, you can vote absentee if you like."

Last to leave was the Big A. He stood in the doorway looking around at our shattered cottage. The busted studs and shards of wood that once were our stairs. A haze of crushed drywall floated in the air as Art lingered, taking it all in.

He was so enormous he filled the entire door jamb. I felt like apologizing, but what could I say? 'Sorry I thought you were a murderer?' Suddenly I couldn't find any words that fit together. It was as if I'd never spoken English at all.

"You know..." he began, "if you're looking for an explanation for all this, maybe you should start next door."

He nodded his big head in the direction of Harold's cottage. "Seems to me a guy with 10,000 Keep Out signs might have something to hide. You know, the one with enough dirt piled up in his backyard to build a land-bridge to outer space? Ever seen that guy step foot in the water? What kind of weirdo lives on a lake and doesn't swim? It's like living in Vegas and not betting the house from time to time. If he wanted to scare somebody off, would have been pretty easy for old Harold to sabotage a bunch of stuff up here during the winter. You know, when nobody would be around to see him doing it, considering he is the only one who lives on the lake year round."

Harold. The name sucked all the air from my lungs. As Art Guilafante turned and left our cottage, I couldn't help but think just how right he was. How right he was and how wrong I'd been.

Eric Walker Williams

29
~~~~~~~

When the sun rose the next morning, I woke up with too many unanswered questions.

Had I somehow overlooked the obvious? Art's voice kept running through my head. It was true Harold was one of the few who actually lived year round on the lake. This meant he had access to our cottage at all times of the day and night. It would have been super easy for him to rig stuff to collapse when nobody was around.

I had been so worried about Art being around after all the accidents, but Harold had been there too. Peering around the corner of our cottage or squinting through the rails of his redwood fence. My skin began to crawl as I remembered telling Harold all about Operation Cowbird. That was really dumb. We hadn't given him a second look, but now it was starting to make sense. Harold had been so quick to point a finger at the Big A.

My mind jumped to meeting him that first night. The way he'd asked if we were going to sell our cottage. Mom was right, that was a strange thing to ask people you hadn't seen in years. Somehow it made total sense now. I couldn't believe how stupid I'd been at every turn. How could I have trusted a man who was so strange in every way? From that awkward smile to his creepy mannerisms to that mountain of dirt he was piling up behind his cottage, it had all been right there before me and I'd missed it. A strange feeling came over me. He'd been right in front of us the whole time. It had been the snaggle-toothed Weird Harold Farcus all along.

Everything Art said made sense to me, and now I needed answers. There was one tiny problem of course. If I was to get answers, there was only one place to find them. I had to ask Harold himself. With everyone busy packing up, I decided to make my move. Kyle shook me off when I asked him to come along, "Wait until tomorrow, I'll go over there with you then."

I crept over to Harold's redwood fence and stopped to look at his wreck of a yard. His three legged lawn chair sat empty. Harold was nowhere to be found. If I was going to confront him now, I'd have to knock on his door.

Suddenly I wasn't so sure this was a good idea. Harold's KEEP OUT signs seemed to be speaking to me now, shouting out their warnings to go away. The statue of the Virgin Mary was holding her arms open as if to say, 'Why, my child? Why would you cross the fence?'

Then, standing there at the edge of Harold's yard, I was back in the water with Grandpa Tug. Those skis felt so awkward. Each outweighed me on their own. Keeping them together was the hardest thing I'd ever done. Grandpa Tug must have felt me shaking because he pulled me closer, whispering in my ear, *"If you're going to make it anywhere in life, Jitterbug, you've gotta learn to face your fears"*.

The rope tightened with Grandpa shouting, "Sit on the chair! Sit on the chair!" as the roar of the boat pulled me

Eric Walker Williams

away. Soon enough I'd fallen over, but instead of yelling at me for failing, Grandpa had been quick to pick me up.

Now I heard his voice again, *'You've got to face your fears'.* I eased a leg over the fence and gently set one foot down in the grass on Harold's side, fully expecting to be swallowed into a hole deep enough to reach China, or at the very least greeted by alarm bells and flashing lights.

With both feet over, I weaved around the empty five gallon buckets and bait coolers. Harold's front door was battered and weathered. It looked just as tired and weak as its owner. I took a deep breath and knocked. Flakes of peeling paint fell away, floating to the ground.

I knocked harder, causing the door to fall open. A blast of spearmint rushed over my face.

"Harold?" There was no answer. This really came as no surprise considering it probably was the first time anyone had knocked on Harold's door since the house had been built.

I paused to consider my options. I could turn around now and live a happy, full life as a celebrated ornithologist making history by discovering an entirely new species of bird, or I could stay here, hoping to find answers to the mystery I'd been trying to solve all week. The answers, if there were any, lay beyond the door. That meant, if I was really going to figure this whole thing out, I had to go inside.

Glancing down toward the water, I checked for Harold one last time. There was nobody there. Only Grandpa Tug's lopsided silver maple, and, beyond that, the greenish-yellow Indian grass listing in the breeze.

Without thinking, I spun around and stepped inside. The cottage was dark. A musty smell hung in the air. The fireplace mantle was covered with taxidermy. A long eared owl, wings spread out and beak flared, stood next to a mink crawling on a log, face wrinkled, teeth bared.

The floor was littered with old issues of *Outdoor Life* and faded fishing jig packages. Light through the picture window lit up a haze of dust floating in the room. Larry was there, standing at attention on his craggy limb, keeping watch over the lake.

Though I would never tell Kyle, a small part of me felt like asking Larry where Harold was. Something told me he knew. Something told me he knew a lot. Whoever was going around sabotaging all our stuff, Larry had seen them. He did have one of the best views of Bass Lake, after all. If only he weren't dead.

Harold's wreck of a living room included two empty recliners. Each flanked one end of a flower print couch. Sagging and misshapen, the cushions were torn at the seams, and one even had a sharp edged spring erupting through a tear in the fabric.

Every step I took was marked by the sound of something being crushed beneath my feet: candy bar wrappers, pieces of dried up food, plastic silverware, Styrofoam plates, and page after page of yellowed newspapers.

"Harold?" I called again.

Stopping to listen, there was no response. There were no sounds inside the cottage save the blood pulsing through my veins. Outside, the coughing of a boat motor trying to start could be heard. Down the hall I found Harold's kitchen. Dishes stacked a foot high littered the counter. A half dozen cereal boxes lay open, some on their sides having spilled their guts out on the dining room table.

Through a grimy window in his mud room, the mound of dirt Harold was creating came into sharp focus. Dad had started calling it 'Mt. Farcus'. The disarray of the house was a bit unsettling, but what I saw next almost made my heart leap from my chest.

There on the kitchen table, between an empty box of Toasty O's and a tackle box that had vomited its contents everywhere, sat a chainsaw. Harold had it pulled apart and appeared to be cleaning it, or maybe fixing it. There was no way to tell.

It was laid out on a bed of newspaper surrounded by tools, a container of bar oil, and dozens of stray parts. The machine looked like it had exploded. Still, nothing could change one simple fact. I was looking at a chainsaw.

Staring at the saw set my neck on fire. Could it have been Harold all along? My mind flashed to him sawing the limb of Grandpa Tug's silver maple just enough to collapse under someone's weight. I could see him notching the shed door supports and the frame of Grandpa's lookout tower.

There was no reason to hang around. I'd seen enough. It had been Weird Harold all along. As much as I hated to admit it, Art Guilafante was right.

It was time to go. I had to get out of there before Harold showed up. Turning back toward the living room, I bolted for the door. Halfway across the room a flash of light caught my eye. It was a small trophy resting proudly on an end table.

Something made me stop to pick it up. It was a golden Large Mouth Bass glued to a wooden block. The inscription was faded and hard to read. I turned it toward the window for better light.

"That one's from '64," a scratchy voice explained, breaking the silence of the room. I turned to the doorway and found Weird Harold Farcus filling it. "Won First place at the Bass Lake Fishing Derby," he announced with pride.

"Caught a four pound speckled bass with a Retro Rocket Jig…seems like yesterday."

I couldn't move. Every muscle in my body was frozen. Time stood still. Harold wasn't moving either. He stayed in the doorway, sure to remain strategically positioned between me and the only way out of his cottage, between me and the only path to freedom, between me and the only chance I had at surviving my summer.

"My daddy…he loved to fish," Harold explained as I set the trophy back carefully. "Momma made a mean catfish stew. Between her garden and daddy huntin' squirrels around the swamp, we always had plenty of food to make it through the winters."

My heart was pounding so hard I could barely hear the man. My head became filled with the roar of his chainsaw. It was just like Weird Harold not to ask why I was there. Normal people would want to know why I had come into their cottage uninvited. It was the most logical question for this situation, and yet he didn't seem to understand this at all.

I felt myself sinking deeper into the depths of Harold's weirdness. It was like jungle quicksand, the more you tried to figure it out, the deeper you were sucked in and the weirder things got.

"Daddy taught me everything I know about jigs and trot lines," Harold went on. "He died in the winter of '83."

My eyes fell on a black and white photo of a young Harold standing next to a small girl. Shirtless and grinning from ear to ear, Harold looked happy, yet even at a young age he was still sporting a miniature white bucket hat.

"I had a younger sister….Lilly. We were best friends. Sunrise to sunset, we did everything together… Fishin', crawdad huntin', trackin' stuff along shore. Drowned when she was eight." Harold's head swung down as the life faded from his beady eyes.

At that moment he wasn't in the living room anymore. He was someplace else. The 1960's maybe, running through the grass with his sister, hand in hand, smiling under a big round summer sun. "Drowned at eight..." he continued as a forlorn look swept over his face, "and I haven't stepped foot in the lake since."

Why was he telling me this? Why didn't he just go get his chainsaw and get this over with already? I wanted to run. I wanted to scream. I wanted to ask Harold if it had been him all along trying to scare us off the lake, but you guessed it, my mind and body were fighting again.

Suddenly I saw Harold's wall for the first time. It was covered with dozens of framed black and white photos. How had I missed them? There were scenes of Harold as a child waterskiing and playing in the lake, pictures of Weed Farcus and his son proudly holding up a line of fish. There was another of Harold as a young boy, skiing with one foot in his ski and one holding the rope, arms extended as if he were about to take flight.

"I used to love the water," he admitted. "Now I can't go near it."

On the wall there was a faded blue ribbon that read 'Champion of the Bass Lake Lawnmower Race-1970' and another for 'Longest Fish in the Bass Lake Festival Fishing Derby- 1961'. There was even a faded photo of a three-year-old Harold trying to tug his first white bucket hat on.

"Some people think I'm a bit weird for that, you know, living on a lake and all, but this is home, always has been and always will be."

More pictures caught my eye. Harold with his mother, one in the kitchen and another of them hanging laundry behind the cottage. There were no strange looks on little Weird Harold's face. He looked like any normal, freckle-faced kid in a white bucket hat, but how could it be?

Suddenly I realized how completely wrong it is for a person to walk into someone else's house uninvited. Sneaking into Harold's cottage was worse than going through Art's shed. It was like going through Art's shed times a million, which isn't good, I mean, even Alison Camarillo can do that math. But it was more than that. Once again, just when he'd seemed to be at his weirdest, Harold found a way to appear normal to me.

Still I couldn't piece it all together. I needed time to sort all this out, but Harold appeared as though time was the last thing he was willing let me have. He was still standing his ground, blocking the doorway. My mind wrestled with the options. Run the other direction? Confront him? Scream?

Everything ran back to Grandpa Tug and facing my fears. I could hear the engine of Grandpa's Toy surging as the rope drew tight and began dragging me through the water. Those giant skis waving back and forth so clumsily.

That was it. I had to confront Harold. He wasn't going to let me out of his cottage. He had spent a week trying to find a way to get rid of me, and now I had just up and walked into his spider web as if asking him to finish the job. "It wasn't Art," I revealed. Harold's brow bent in a confused manner. "He wasn't behind all the accidents," I continued. "It wasn't him. It was someone else."

Harold didn't answer. He didn't move either. The man's face went black in the doorway as the sun slid out from behind the clouds. Was he considering his options? At least the

Eric Walker Williams

chainsaw was torn apart, so I knew he wouldn't be reaching for that.

He aimed one of his large, scuffed up boots at me and began to step through the doorway. This was it. It was chainsaw time. Why wasn't I running? Why wasn't I screaming?

Then a door slamming in the driveway stopped the man in his tracks. His head spun around. I could tell he didn't like what he saw. Someone was in Weird Harold's driveway.

30

~~~~~~~

"I see him, Larry!" Harold groused. "Calm down already! If you're so darned interested to know who it is, why don't you climb down off that limb and walk your stubby little legs out there yourself?"

Standing there in Harold's living room, surrounded by the madness that was his life, it struck me for the first time how utterly disturbing it was for a grown man to be speaking to a piece of taxidermy.

Larry was still there, looking out at Lake Road faithfully, giving no protest, because he was dead. Still there remained some small part of me that wanted to reach out to Larry. Something about the way he was perched on that limb. There was a quiet strength in those tiny shoulders. I suppose at that point I would have taken help from anyone, be it a stuffed opossum, Roni Bonafetti, or even big Art Guilafante.

What was I doing here? How could I have doubted everyone on the lake? All those who had called Harold weird for all these years? Who was I to think I was the only one who understood Weird Harold Farcus?

Peering past Larry out the picture window, my eyes doubled in size upon spotting what was in the drive. It was the same van I'd seen in the parade, and there on the top stood the same giant ten foot tall, heinous looking insect I'd seen as well.

Eric Walker Williams

We both stood waiting for the driver of the white van. Harold in the doorway, and me staring out the front window over Larry's shoulder. Moving at a snail's pace, a dumpy man in a greasy work suit was making his way toward Harold's porch. A red oval patch on his chest had the name 'Randy' stitched in white letters. Apparently Randy was out of shape because the walk from the truck to the porch had him panting for air. Sweat was beading on his puffy, unshaven cheeks as he stopped at the doorstep. This was my hero? My knight in shining armor?

"Howdy there," Randy huffed. His words were difficult to understand from a mouth full of long leaf tobacco.

Through the window, I took in his frowzy appearance. His wrinkled jumpsuit, so stained with coffee and other unidentified substances it barely looked white anymore. His hair was matted with sweat and stuffed under a mesh hat two sizes too big.

"Whadd'a you need?" Harold muttered.

"Names Randy, of Randy's Extermination," he said, pointing over his shoulder to his little white van, which clearly had 'Randy's Extermination' painted across the hood.

Randy's eyes wandered up to the picture window and locked on Larry for a moment. I tried making eye contact with him over the opossum's shoulder through the window. Rolling my eyes around wildly, I tried signaling the word 'HELP' with them, but Randy just looked at me as if I were a life size bobblehead doll.

He tugged his tool belt up on his waist and spat a long stream of tobacco juice into the dirt before turning his attention to Harold. Never one to give up, I edged closer to the bay window Larry called home. With his frozen body inches from my face, I could smell Larry's musty fur. The word 'help' was on the tip of my tongue when Larry shifted suddenly and scrambled down from his branch. Without making a sound, he darted past me and leapt from the bay window.

I turned and watched as he raced over the empty potato chip bags and jig packages, making his way to Harold's couch where he was quick to seek refuge under it. There was no time for the revelation that Larry was actually alive and well to register before Randy began explaining his arrival.

"Well, figured I'd stop by and check your property, too." Randy squinted up at Harold, his lips creasing to a smile. My eyes bulged upon discovering his teeth were stained brown and dotted with loose flakes of tobacco. A long pause followed. From somewhere came the sound of Art cursing, probably something to do with Bud and Ella again.

Randy shoved a card in Harold's hand. "Randy's Extermination," Harold read aloud, "If your boot ain't big enough to squash it, call me."

"Figured I'd stop by and see if you wanted your place treated too."

The man removed his cap and pushed the sweat riddled tussocks of hair back on his scalp before slamming the hat back in place.

"Treated for what?" Harold asked.

"Well, pert near ever place on the lake has called me but these three cottages over here," Randy explained tugging at his tool belt again. "I figured it was just a matter of time before you guys would be after me too."

"Well, you still ain't told me what you're treatin' for?" Harold demanded.

"Cryptotermes cavifrons." Randy revealed before releasing another long stream of tobacco juice into the drive.

Cryptotermes cavifrons… the words swirled through my head. Cryptotermes cavifrons. It took a minute, but soon enough I had it. And that's when everything came into focus. Cryptotermes cavifrons explained everything! The tree limb, the overhead supports, the lookout, Grandpa's Toy, the grandstands at the lawnmower speedway, the bunk beds, even the banister and staircase. They explained everything.

They also told me Weird Harold wasn't a killer. He was just a strange man living in a run-down house on a tiny lake who loved Keep Out signs and bad fashion. And Larry was real! He wasn't a piece of taxidermy. He'd been playing dead all along because that's what opossums do when they feel threatened. How had I missed it? Harold hadn't been carrying taxidermy around with him all week, Larry was alive and well and Harold Farcus counted him amongst his closest friends.

"'Fraid you're gonna have to speak English mister," Harold answered.

"Termites," I announced out loud, arriving at the door and beating Randy to the punch.

"Nasty little buggers," Randy explained. "Tearin' up properties all over the lake. Bad as I've seen 'em in twenty-five years!"

The name Cryptotermes cavirons had bored its way into my brain. This explained it all. Termites had eaten away everything on the property. They had caused all the accidents. It hadn't been big Art Guilafante and his Too-Big-for-Bass-Lake-Floatplane. It hadn't been Weird Harold Farcus and his Keep Out signs. It had been a bug smaller than the eraser on the end of a pencil.

That explained the oversized bug costume at the goat drop. Randy had driven his van in the parade to advertise there were termites to kill on the lake. Termites explained it all. This dumpy looking, chaw spitting exterminator needed all of thirty seconds to solve a mystery that had baffled Kyle and me all week. A termite problem had explained everything, everything at once.

Suddenly I glanced up at Weird Harold. Harold Farcus, the man I was about to accuse of everything. This helpless, wild-eyed recluse who'd spent his entire life on Bass Lake, he wasn't trying to scare us away. He wasn't a killer. He was just a nosy neighbor with bad fashion and worse teeth.

Harold grew up on the lake just like my father had; I'd seen the pictures. He had strong memories of this place too. In those old photographs I'd seen the life in his eyes and the smile that was so foreign to his leathery face now. He loved Bass Lake. Why did I ever think he would want to keep someone away from a place he loved so dearly?

Suddenly I couldn't believe I'd ever suspected Harold at all. Wasn't this the same man who'd been nothing but a good neighbor to my family for over forty years? The same man who'd sat in his white plastic lawn chair protecting our property while we were back in the city?

As Harold and Randy headed down to his truck to look at something, I raced into the jungle of horseweeds. Beating a path back toward our cottage, I leapt the redwood fence like an Olympic hurdler.

It hadn't been Harold, and while I wasn't impressed with Art tearing my lake up and still thought of him as the King of Blusterstan, it hadn't been him either. Termites explained everything, and now I owed Art an apology, a real apology.

Art had decided to set some land aside for the animals, and that was enough to convince me he was worthy of an apology, the apology my parents had asked me to give last week. I had to apologize for suspecting Art, not only for suspecting him, but for accusing him and for doubting him.

I ran straight through our front yard and didn't stop until I had reached the Guilafante's cottage. Nobody answered the front door, so I headed around back.

"Art?" I called out wandering into his backyard. There was no answer. I stood with my back to his cottage staring into his shed. The access door was standing wide open, but everything beyond it was pitch black. Was he in there? I wasn't about to go back in, not after the full blown trial my parents had put me through the last time.

Silence surrounded me until the scratchy call of a grackle was heard from deep inside a nearby button bush. "It wasn't Harold, Art," I announced. "I was wrong about both of you…" I put a hand up to shield my eyes from the sun. "I just came over to…well…apologize I guess."

Before I could take a step toward the shed something grabbed me from behind. Large, thick and powerful hands clamped over my mouth and wrenched onto my arm. Then, whatever had taken hold of me, began dragging me inside Art's cottage.

I tried to wrestle away, but it was no use. Whatever had me was stronger than an ox. Soon we'd entered the back door of the Guilafante cottage where I was promptly thrown into a kitchen chair. "You've made me wait far too long for this," a deep voice bellowed.

I looked up and found an all too familiar face glaring back at me. One belonging to big Art Guilafante.

31

"You just couldn't leave it alone could you?" Art said, forcing me back into my chair. "Your dad was ready to sell until you started nosin' around! It shouldn't have come to this. It shouldn't have been this hard. All your dad had to do was let me write him a check, throw you guys in the car and everyone would have been just fine, but no, you wouldn't have any of that would you? You had to keep your precious little cottage. You had to go snooping around all week like some nosy FBI agent."

"I thought you weren't after our cottage. You said so yourself," I replied, trying my best to sound shocked that what I had suspected all along was in fact true.

Art pulled a roll of duct tape from the cabinet drawer before jerking my hands behind my back to tape them together. "I have to give you credit, kid. You had most of it sorted out," he admitted. "Sure you missed the mark on a few things—but for the most part you knew what was going on."

"What do you mean?" I asked. "I don't know what you're talking about!"

"Sorry, sweetheart," Art chuckled. "It's far too late in the game to be playing dumb. You're in *way* over your head now."

"But you said you were going to fix our cottage. You offered to help us!"

"Nothing any good neighbor with a three billion dollar construction company wouldn't do. Now offering and actually doing it, well, those are two different stories." Art slithered to his kitchen window to cast a nervous gaze before continuing, "I would have had my crew start in like gangbusters, but at some point they would have found so much mold beneath that old eyesore, they would have walked off the job. See, mold is just way too expensive for most people to deal with. Selling would have been your parents only move."

I shook my head, fighting back tears. "Turns out you were right all along, sweetheart... I wanted your cottage and Harold's too. You knew that. I followed you that day to the goat drop. Remember? I saw you talking with Harold. You told him didn't you? You told him everything."

The word 'everything' caused Art's eyes to flare with rage.

"I have no idea what you're talking about! Please, let me go!!" I shouted in panic. "Just let me go. We're leaving today, and we won't come back. I won't tell anyone, I swear!"

"Your dad's not the brightest bulb in the bunch, but you, well, you're different now aren't you? You were way more than I expected," the Big A seethed. "Guess it's true what they say; dynamite does come in small packages."

Art rolled his blueprints out on the kitchen table. His large eyes wandered over the drawings as I pulled and tugged as hard as I could against the tape. So many layers were wrapped around my wrists, they felt like steel shackles.

I'd been right all along. The whole week flashed before my eyes. They hadn't been accidents at all. My mind went back to the day in the shed when Art had arrived. How he'd found Kyle and me lying under that door. The way he'd rattled off all the things that could have happened to us, how the shed door could have given Kyle a concussion or fractured his skull. It could have punctured his lung or broken his spine. Art had run down that list of possibilities as if he'd spent a lot of time considering them. In fact, he fired them off like someone who had planned on the shed door falling the whole time.

Now this was real. Art had been stalking me like big game all week, and now he had me dead in his sights. This wasn't a game. This wasn't a detective show. Art Guilafante was really going to hurt me. Despite all this, I wasn't about to go down without a fight.

"You weren't really going to build a wildlife refuge were you? That was a lie, too, wasn't it?"

"Nature's a nuisance, kid. A boundary to economic progress," Art declared, his lips creasing into a wicked smile, "but I plan to change all that." He planted a finger near the edge of the lake. "The golf course is here, and after we drain the swamp, the backside of the golf course will be there. And this…" he dragged his large round finger across an empty space I guessed to be the lake before stopping sharply, "this is your precious Minnix family cottage," I could read the devious look in his eyes and braced for what was coming. "It's where my amusement park will be."

"Amusement park?"

The Big A threw his shoulders back as his chest swelled up like a frigate bird. "Art World," he declared with pride.

"Art World?" I choked. "That sounds like a place you'd go to buy a cheap painting for your house or something."

The man's big face wrinkled with disappointment. Right up until the end it would seem my mouth was once again too quick for my brain.

"Well, we're still playing with the name," he revealed, somewhat embarrassed. "Anyway, just picture it, people paying money hand over fist for a chance to ride roller coasters, eat cotton candy, and take a spin on a ferris wheel so tall you can see clear back to Chicago. It'll be a cash cow."

"Because," I said robotically, "amusement parks make money."

His eyes flashed like gold doubloons. "Your family is the only thing standing between me and Art World. So once you disappear, there's no way your parents will ever want to come back here. See, the only thing a parent fears more than mold in a house is a missing child. They'll sell for sure. And they'll sell to me because I'm such a great guy-what with the way I showed up to help every time you were nearly killed, and not to mention the nature preserve I originally promised, but will never follow through on. Then I'll elbow Farcus out of the way and smash down those two eyesores next door to make room for...*Art World*."

"No," I answered quickly. "They'll know it was you. My parents believed me all along," I bluffed. "There's no way you'll get away with it."

"Really?" Art responded with a wicked grin, "Well, after you disappear, Sheriff Carlson will start asking questions, and I'll just have to show him the picture I took a few minutes ago. The one of you standing next to Weird Harold in the doorway of his cottage. It'll be enough to throw them off my trail and cook old Harold's goose as well." My heart sank. "it will be the last known photograph of you and they'll broadcast it on every TV news station from here to Bangkok.

And when Farcus gets arrested, he'll need money for all his legal fees. If only there were a really quick way for him to come up with the cash. Any ideas?"

My head dropped again, "Sell his cottage."

"Of course, it won't matter in the end. He can have all the money in the world, but between you missing and the photograph, there isn't a lawyer on earth that will be able to keep a guy that weird out of jail."

A quiet moment lingered as Art waited for me to put it together. The sound of a jet ski tearing across the lake buzzed through the window. My head hung like a whipped dog.

"I really did like you, Kayla. You're very bright, and you've shown a lot of moxie. You also have passion, and it takes passion to make it big in this world," Art said, glancing nervously out the window.

"You remind me of myself when I was younger, except you're a girl, and I could care less about animals and, oh yeah, I never played with dolls or was much for coloring books. Something about staying inside the lines drove me crazy. See, even at a young age, I wanted to make my own lines."

"What about Taryn? She told you she loved the swamp!"

Art's face seemed to brighten to a near blush, "Yeah, I made that part up. She hated every minute of that place. Taking her there was a bold move on your part, unfortunately sometimes being bright and bold is a combination that can get a little girl into trouble. So you and I are going to take a little plane ride, and nobody will *ever* see you again." Art seethed, eyes full of fire.

Gone was the teddy bear face I'd seen yesterday. He looked every bit the sinister monster I'd suspected him of being all along. I'd been right about big Art Guilafante from the first moment I met him.

"Ever been to northern Canada?" he asked.

The man threw a duffle bag onto the table. It didn't take Sherlock Holmes to realize what the bag was for. It seemed just large enough to squeeze a nosy young girl inside, a nosy young girl who loved nature, happened to be a twin and really hated obnoxiously large floatplanes.

"Don't worry, few have," Art went on, "but trust me when I say it's beautiful in July and has all kinds of creepy crawly things I'm sure you're going to love counting or watching or whatever it is you do with them. See, in a way I'm doing you a favor. You can spend the rest of your life surrounded by the things you love most. Best of all, it's only a few hours from here by plane. I should be back before sunset. Notice I said *I* should be back before sunset."

"Let me guess, it's less than a thousand miles, so the otter can make it without refueling?"

"Like I said," the man answered, his face spreading into another devilish grin, "you're a smart girl, just not smart enough to leave things well enough alone."

He threw himself into wrapping my ankles up in tape. I got dizzy watching the spool spiraling around my legs. He must have wrapped them twenty times. Before he could say anything else, a knock came from the door.

Art looked at me. Apparently he could read the look on my face because he stripped off another piece of tape and stuck it over my mouth before I could scream. "Be right back. Don't go anywhere," he said giving me a wicked wink while leaving to answer the door.

It seemed like it took a year for Art to reach it, but when he finally opened the door, I heard a familiar voice.

It wasn't the President again or my father. It wasn't Harold Farcus or the Sheriff either. It was Randy the Exterminator, my somewhat overweight, chaw spitting, knight in shining armor.

"Termites!" I heard Art repeat with shock.

I tried wiggling out of the tape again, but it was simply too tight. That's when I noticed the back door standing open. I jumped up on my feet and tried hopping for the door but soon lost my balance and fell over.

There was no way I could get back to my feet now. I tried wriggling like a gartner snake but could only move sideways. Meanwhile Art was trying his best to get rid of Randy, "Why don't you come back tomorrow, and we'll talk about it some more. I'm in the middle of something important right now."

Art was in the middle of something all right, in the middle of flying me off to some remote part of the world where he would leave me to die alone in the wilderness.

"Well, I'd just like to get you signed up now, so I can get all three cottages over here done when I come back in the morning," a determined Randy responded. "Look, it'll take five minutes to fill the paperwork out. If you do it now, I'll give you half off the regular price!"

Art started in on Randy, blathering on about how a man who owned a floatplane and had a Segway in his living room didn't need half off the regular price. Art said he would write a check right now if that meant Randy would take a long walk off a short pier. Somehow my mind became lost in the droning sound of a nearby lawnmower.

I decided there was so much I still wanted to do. It couldn't end like this. I wanted to work with endangered species. I wanted to lobby on Capitol Hill for animal rights and discover a new species of bird. I also hoped to turn thirteen at some point. I had plans and places I wanted to go, and none of them involved winding up in the remote Canadian wilderness zipped up in a duffle bag.

That's when another knock was heard. My eyes darted to the back door, but it was empty. I could hear Art. He was still at the front door, trying to get rid of Randy. Three more knocks followed. Where were they coming from?

As I lay with my face pressed against Art's cold linoleum floor, the knocking grew louder. Somehow it seemed to be coming from beneath my cheek, but how could that be? Did Art have someone tied up under his cottage? Could it be Jimmy Longstockings?

I jerked my head away as something broke through the floor, missing my face by inches. Shards of wood shot into the air as the linoleum peeled away. That's when I saw the head of a shovel force its way through the kitchen floor.

32

The shovel moved around, breaking more wood and linoleum loose until it had created a large hole in the floor.
That's when I first saw it. A most strange, yet quite familiar
and definitely welcome sight. It was the white bucket hat of
Weird Harold Farcus, rising through the floor.

Harold didn't have to speak. We both knew what the
other was thinking as he ripped the tape from my mouth.

"The table!" I shrieked pointing with my head. "Grab
the blueprints, hurry!"

Harold rose out of the hole and snatched the papers.
He grabbed a steak knife from a caddy on the counter and
cut me loose.

"Hurry up. Get in the hole," he whispered, in the way
only Harold could.

My feet paused at the edge of the hole. Going in meant
I trusted Harold. It meant I trusted the one man on the
lake everyone feared was hiding something; the ivory billed
woodpecker of Bass Lake. It also meant I trusted the man I
fully believed was trying to kill me only a half hour before.

The hole looked tiny, as if you couldn't even roll a basketball down it. Could I really squeeze through? Then for some reason my thoughts flashed to Larry. The Virginia opossum Harold kept in his front window. He was about the size of a house cat, but opossums were notorious for squeezing into small spaces. One time I'd read a full grown opossum could fit through a hole smaller than a softball. Still, the tunnel looked tight.

As I stood weighing my options, I heard Art's front door slam shut. There was nothing left to consider. I threw myself down the hole.

What I found was a passageway leading back to Weird Harold's cottage. The man had actually dug a tunnel from his property, completely under our cottage and all the way over to the Big A's kitchen.

We weren't halfway back when we heard Art's voice booming down the tunnel from his kitchen. Then the sounds of him scrabbling into the tunnel could be heard. The Big A was coming after us. The darkness was blinding, but there was only one way to go. Away from Art. Harold and I crawled as fast as we could. I kept the blueprints folded under my arm as Art's shouting grew louder. He was getting closer.

The tunnel came up inside the mud room of Harold's cottage. There I was happy to breathe the musty smells and walk upon empty potato chip sacks again. Still, we had to do deal with Art Guilafante somehow.

"Do something! He's coming!" I shouted.

Harold walked out his back door and quickly returned with a large cage. It was a wire Have-a-Heart trap, and inside it was a large ball of black fur. It wasn't just any large ball of black fur, it was the same one that had been the scourge of Bass Lake for generations. For when Harold set the cage on the floor, Tricky the make-up wearing, trash eating, shin-splitting, staircase-shattering raccoon spun around and glared up at the two of us.

"Caught him last night, rummagin' through the garbage…after all these years."

"It's not surprising he was after your garbage," I answered. "The surprising thing is you caught him! What did you use? Old cheeseburger? Peanut butter and jelly?"

"Naw. Used some of mother's old eye liner," Harold confessed with a wink. "Know what happens when you get coons stuck in a tight place?"

"Grandpa Tug always said they don't want to hurt you," I answered quickly, "unless you get them cornered!"

Harold opened the door of the trap and Tricky bounded into the tunnel, scurrying away from us and toward Big Art Guilafante. I'll never forget the sound that followed. Art was screaming like a little girl, well, a little girl who was six foot seven and weighed in at around 300 pounds that is. Still, 300 pounds or not, Tricky was hissing and cackling and barking as he chased Art all the way back to his cottage.

As it turned out, Harold had been tunneling all along, which explained the mound of dirt and the midnight digging sessions. Though he'd convinced me to go after them, Harold planned on finding his own way to Art's blueprints too, just in case. And while I was busy trying to find a reason Harold Farcus would want to rip a cottage away from my family, or scare us off the lake, he'd been busy trying to save us from the Big A.

Harold's warning, the one that had sent my mind racing that first night, had been simply that, a warning. 'I'd hate to see a little girl like you get hurt'. It had seemed totally creepy at the time, but it wasn't him foreshadowing the fact he wanted to hurt me. It was his way of protecting me. He said watching my brother and I running around was like watching home movies. We were a sequel to Harold and Lilly. Losing Lilly had changed Harold's life forever and he didn't want Kyle to suffer the same loss.

Carl Carlson, the Sheriff of California County, was waiting for Art at his cottage when he fought his way out of Harold's hole. Seems Weird Harold had called the Sheriff before setting off to rescue me. It took one phone call to the mayor's office for my dad to find out Art was already the target of an FBI investigation. The Feds were on the lake before Tricky could find his way out of Harold's tunnel. Of course when the men showed up with 'FBI' on the back of their jackets, we had to explain to Abby that 'FBI' stood for Federal Bureau of Investigation and not Fijian Boomerang Instructors.

We gladly turned the blueprints over to the FBI. They told us Jimmy Longstockings' dog wasn't the only one who'd turned up missing. Nobody had seen Jimmy either, at least not since Art had moved in. The Big A had planned on tearing our cottages down all along, and when Jimmy had said no, Art made the poor man an offer he couldn't refuse. Well, at least that's how Kyle put it.

It turned out Harold was a millionaire after all and his family owned all the land in and around the swamp. The Farcus family had been the largest supplier of mint to Wrigley for over 100 years. Harold was quick to agree the swamp should become a nature preserve. He even decided to name it the 'Tug Minnix Nature Sanctuary'. While I plan to spend most days there, making notes and counting birds, I'm not the only one who will love the new preserve. We were able to catch Tricky again and relocate him to the swamp. From what I could tell, he thinks it's a pretty excellent place to catch crawfish, and believe me, Dad was thankful for that.

Harold and I organized the first annual 'Weed Farcus Memorial Fishing Derby' and Harold even offered to give a free fishing clinic for young kids. Of course, he did it all from the safety of shore with Larry nuzzled at his feet.

The President wasn't interested in answering Sheriff Carlson's questions. This came as no surprise, because if there are two things politicians are good at, its dodging questions and pretending environmental issues will eventually work themselves out. When the FBI got involved however, the President was quick to tell them all about Art's plans to swindle our properties. Turns out Wilbert Harley was the largest investor of them all in 'Art World'.

My parents didn't sell the cottage. In fact we came back the next year. It was Harold who said change is inevitable. It's what you do with it that matters and I suppose those words describe Bass Lake perfectly now.

You can't stop change. You can't prevent it either. All you can do is find a way to deal with it. It really is what you do with change that matters. Sure, Art thought he could change the lake. Tear down a few cottages, put up a few condos, but in the end he really couldn't. He built bigger homes and a nine-hole golf course, but try as he may, even the Big A and all his money couldn't change tiny Bass Lake.

Bud and Ella had faced Art's changes. They'd suffered several attacks from the Big A, which forced the rebuilding of their nest on more than one occasion. Despite all the change, swallows by the dozens will still use their little wings to return to Bass Lake from South America every spring.

The people on the lake were dealing with change too. Art Guilafante had done his best to redevelop it. Tearing down family cottages and ripping out trees to make way for golf courses, parking lots and plastic condos, but even with the expensive condos and four star restaurants, Bass Lake was still a family lake. It would just have some new families on it. Despite all the changes, the same happy families will come back to sit under the same summer sun. It doesn't matter how many condos or golf courses there are on the lake, fathers and grandfathers will still teach their kids to ski on her crystal blue waters.

Art needed money to cover his court costs after losing his business, so he sold his cottage to a nice family named Messerschmitt. I didn't mind them because they seemed normal and had a daughter named Lizzie who wasn't afraid of the swamp. In fact Lizzie was with me the morning I finally found a glossy ibis. We heard him long before we saw him. Like a squeaky porch swing or my brother practicing for music class on his recorder, out of nowhere the call of the ibis filled the swamp. When I parted the reeds in front of us, there he was. Standing in the shallows, the sun bouncing off his purple back.

"Glory be!" a shrill voice rattled from behind us. It was the Trash Queen, in all her gaudy glory. "You did it, dearie!

You finally did it!" she shouted, waving her double barrel over her head like a cowboy.

Change had hit me like a haymaker, too. I knew now Grandpa Tug was gone and nothing could ever bring him back. I also decided he wouldn't want me just sitting around missing him all the time. He'd want me to enjoy the lake. He'd also want me to learn to ski.

Dad bought a new wakeboard boat that summer, one that sounds like the Space Shuttle when it takes off. He christened it 'Walter's Toy' and, after agreeing to buy a new muffler and not drive past the rookeries, I agreed to let him take me skiing.

The water felt warm, and the skis were somehow much lighter than I'd remembered. I felt naked in the water without Grandpa there. Dad steered the boat around, slowly taking slack out of the rope. The line drew tight and my pulse quickened. Dad hit the throttle and the rope jerked me hard against the water. I bent my knees like I was on a chair and slowly rose to the top of the wake.

The wind rippled through my hair as the shoreline raced by. Turning my head, I saw my new friends watching from shore. Bud and Ella flitting around the Indian grass, Harold in his three legged lawn chair and Larry looking on from his perch in the front window. I waved to them.

High above, puffy white clouds gazed down at me. I knew Grandpa Tug was sitting on the edge of one watching, probably blowing the steam from his coffee and thinking of another bad joke. He was proud of me for finally staying on the chair, for finding that ibis, and for moving on. After all, there was no way his little Jitterbug could just sit still all summer. The lake was too beautiful, too magical of a place to go around thinking your neighbors are up to no good.

Eric Walker Williams

I realize now, neighbors are simply people who want the same things as you; especially at the lake. To laugh and live and enjoy time away from their busy lives. That's all neighbors are. They're no different than you or me, and we shouldn't go around accusing them of being anything else. Wait a minute, is that Mr. Messerschmitt trying to open our new shed door?

THE END

About the Author

Eric Walker Williams is a children's writer, husband, father, and pretty good American. He wrote his first story at age eight on a manual typewriter so heavy he couldn't even pick it up.

In addition to a weekly newspaper column in *The Lebanon Reporter*, Eric's work has been featured in *Faces* the Magazine, *The Indianapolis Star*, and various online publications. Learn more about his writing at ericwalkerwilliams.com or at facebook.com/EricWalkerWilliams.

Special Thanks...

Special thanks go to the Johnsons and Rusnaks for sharing their perfect little world with me for all those years. Thank you to Mikesch Muecke for your patience and being the first to take a chance. Ever diligent and equally honest, special thanks as well to Dr. Charlie Fisher, Kary Ann Hill (the Queen of Oxford), and Steve Tearman. Thanks also go to Kimberly and the kids, you boys are an inspiration each day. Double-secret, super-special thanks go to Muscatatuck and all those wild places everywhere.

AMAZE YOUR FRIENDS!

STAGE YOUR OWN iBiS SiGHTiNG!

JUST LIKE KAYLA!

Go to Eric's website and look for the "Find a Glossy Tab" to get started!

ERIC'S TOP BIRDING TIPS

1 Note the size of the bird. Is it larger than a robin or smaller?

Look for special markings on the bird: A wing bar, eye stripe etc. **2**

3 Where did you see the bird? Near water, open field, in the woods.

CONTACT ERIC TODAY!

ON FACEBOOK:

Eric Walker Williams

WEBSITE:

www.ericwalkerwilliams.com

www.ingramcontent.com/pod-product-compliance
Lightning Source LLC
Chambersburg PA
CBHW060550260626
47161CB00003B/1140